When Bat was a Bird

and other Animal Tales from Africa

told by Nick Greaves
illustrated by David du Plessis

THIS BOOK IS DEDICATED, WITH LOVE, TO MY SON,
DOUGLAS. THANKS FOR BEING A GREAT GUINEA PIG!

Contents

Author's Note

The twenty-four stories in this book are drawn from the lore and mythology of a number of southern African tribal groupings, each with its own language and traditional lifestyle, its customs, convictions and courtesies.

The groups, separated by geography and history, are clearly quite different in character. Not so obvious, perhaps, are their affinities, the cultural connections between them and even with peoples far to the north – links forged during the centuries of slow migration, merging and mixing that produced modern Africa's current human landscape. The shared heritage is most evident, perhaps, in the realm of oral literature. Many of the legends and tales that the storytellers have passed down from generation to generation have basic similarities. A familiar character in most societies, for example, is the trickster, a wily individual and a creature well known to the people of the area. Thus the crafty jackal of Zulu folklore can be compared to the prankster hare of Shona fable (which in turn has his direct counterpart in the African-American Brer Rabbit slave stories) and even to the cunning spider of the Efe, or Pygmies, of the equatorial rainforests. The tale may have different physical characters, but the basic theme and the outcome are invariably the same.

There are literally thousands of stories that make up the canon of oral fiction, and the tapestry is both intricate and rich. But it represents the old Africa, and unhappily the tales are being lost to us as urban communities expand and the modern world takes over. The fictional characters – the animals, reptiles and birds so well known to and intimately involved with the rural African societies of yesteryear – are also disappearing. Hunters and poachers are taking a devastating toll, rainforests are being destroyed; once-fertile parts of the African countryside are turning to desert, the farm lands are spreading as populations increase, alien plant life is encroaching, and the habitats – the broad sunlit spaces that once supported such a splendid number and variety of life forms – are shrinking.

There is, however, some light on the horizon. The people of Africa are conscious of the wealth and beauty of their wildlife legacy, and of the value of their remaining wildernesses. Governments are investing heavily in conservation. Existing wildlife areas are being upgraded and new ones created by the year, some of them, the so-called 'peace parks', established across international frontiers in order to free up the land for the more wide-ranging animals, to restore to them their ancient migratory routes.

The retelling of these few tales, most of them about the animals of the African bush, will, I hope, help to preserve a little of that vanishing past for our children, and also reinforce, however modestly, the growing awareness of Africa's fragile and infinitely precious natural heritage.

NICK GREAVES

Why Monkey fears Leopard

A NDEBELE TALE

One day, long ago, Ingwe the leopard was sprawled along the spreading branches of a pod mahogany tree and gazing at his reflection in the pool below. Ingwe was very particular about his appearance: he spent more time admiring himself than any other animal in the bush. As a consequence, he was generally considered the handsomest animal in the wild.

Now Ingwe had been so self-absorbed in studying his immaculate appearance that he forgot all about Mpisi, the spotted hyaena, who was waiting to see him. Eventually the hyaena made a small giggling noise to attract the leopard's attention and remind him of their appointment. Ingwe was jolted out of his daydream and remembered that the hyaena was patiently hanging about. He stood up, lazily stretched his body and jumped down the tree in one fluid motion.

'Well, what is it?' asked Ingwe, curious as to why Mpisi had asked to see him.

'News,' said the hyaena, as he trotted forward to meet the leopard. 'Baboon has found a huge, strange gourd full of water in the forest. He is offering a reward to anyone that can drink it all in one day!'

'Oh! That sounds easy enough. Is that all there is to this urgent meeting?' said Ingwe disdainfully.

'Yes, that is all,' replied the hyaena, somewhat put out by the leopard's nonchalance.

'Hmm!' mused Ingwe thoughtfully for a while. 'Where did Baboon find this unusual gourd of water?' he eventually asked.

'No one knows for sure. Some say it came from the human village on the other side of the great river.'

'Indeed? Then I think I will go and see what the commotion is all about. I thank you for having the sense and the manners to notify me of this event. I am much obliged.'

'My pleasure, I assure you!' Mpisi grinned with delight, then trotted off down towards the river to give the news to Mvuu, the hippopotamus.

Ingwe stalked off in the direction of the forest and it was only after several hours of travel that he arrived in a large clearing. It was evident that something unusual was afoot. An extraordinary event, apparently, had brought together a great many of the animals of the bush, and more kept arriving. In the centre of the clearing was a huge old baboon, sitting with one of his daughters. Next to them was an enormous gourd filled with a clear liquid, and it was this that everyone was staring at.

For a moment Ingwe surveyed the scene with dignity, then he walked over to his friend Isilwane, the lion, and enquired if he knew any more about the mysterious challenge.

'Just an ordinary gourd of water as far as I know,' Isilwane replied. 'They say there is a prize for anyone who can drink it all in one day. Ridiculous I say! I could drink it in one hour!'

'Absurdly easy!' sneered the leopard. 'I reckon I could drink it in three-quarters of that time. I shall win the prize!'

'You have not won yet!' snorted the lion indignantly. 'When I said an hour I actually meant half an hour. Rest assured that I shall win!'

'And what good would such a boast be?' said Mvuu, the hippopotamus, as he waddled up to join them. 'I can beat you all easily! What is a gourd of water to me? It is a mere mouthful! I will gulp it all down in one go and not even notice it.'

The same argument was raging all over the clearing, and the volume of sound rose as the voices became quite heated. Suddenly Ndwanguli, the baboon, shouted above the growing clamour, and silence descended on the gathering. Baboon confirmed that the rules were, first, that the gourd had to be drunk in one day and the individual to do so would be the winner and, second, that lots would be drawn to see who would be the first contestant.

After a great deal of excitement it was Mvuu, the hippopotamus, who won with the shortest straw. The crowd hushed as the hippo walked up to the gourd. Looking very confident, as well he might, he took a deep breath and put his mouth to the cool, clear liquid.

A moment later a huge roar shattered the silence of the clearing and the gathering was amazed to see Mvuu leap wildly into the air and start dancing up and down on the spot. How he roared, bellowed and howled! With tears streaming from his little eyes he tore off down the pathway towards the river and began frantically washing out his mouth. The liquid from the gourd, though it looked like water, had stung and burnt Mvuu like nothing that he had ever tried before.

This was not surprising, for the liquid was a gourd of *katchass*, a brew of powerful liquor that had somehow been stolen from the human village not too far away.

The animals knew nothing of such things, and there was another round of noisy chatter and argument, and indeed a good deal of mirth over Mvuu's distress. Ingwe was secretly pleased, for he thought, as did many other animals, that the competition would be over before it started. After all, Mvuu was the obvious contender to win. But now Ingwe felt that he really could win and he stepped forward to take his turn.

Silence once again fell on the clearing as Ingwe approached the gourd. All eyes were upon him as he paused for breath, and then took a gulp of 'water'. There was an instant's pause and then Ingwe was also howling and dancing on the spot. He too thought that his tongue was on fire and so he raced off down to the river to wash his mouth.

Lion was next. He drew the gourd to his mouth, and then ran to the river, as did all the other animals that tried to drink the *katchass*.

Eventually Inkawu, the little vervet monkey, walked up to the baboon from a patch of long grass and said he would like to try. But he asked if he could lie down and rest between each mouthful, provided that the gourd was completed down to the last drop before the day was done, just as the rules stated. Baboon and the remaining animals conferred and quickly agreed that the little monkey's proposal did fulfil all the requirements.

Inkawu ran straight up to the gourd, took a sip, and ran back to the grass from whence he came. Every few minutes he would run back to the gourd for another sip, and within a couple of hours the gourd was half empty. Already the little monkey had done what none of the other great beasts of the bush could do, and he had done it by making over a hundred brief visits!

Just as the sun was setting the monkey ran up for the last time and the last few drops of the fiery liquid were consumed.

Most of the animals that had tried to drink the firewater had returned from the river to see whether the monkey could succeed where they had failed. Ingwe, sitting in a nearby tree, was amazed at how the little monkey could possibly stand such torment. But as he stared at the long grass, he sensed something moving. At first he thought that it might be a trick of the failing light. But the more intently he looked – and we know that the leopard has remarkably good eyesight – the more certain he felt that something was moving. In fact several things were moving! No, lots and lots of things were moving! It was the tails of dozens and dozens of vervet monkeys waving in the long grass.

At that moment, loud applause broke out as the crafty little monkey was draining the last drop of 'water' and apparently winning the competition, none the worse for wear. In the excitement, no one had noticed the waving monkey tails in the long grass, nor did they see Ingwe sneak out of his tree and stalk the patch of grass. Nor did the gathering of monkeys notice. Then the leopard pounced.

'Cheats! Frauds! Liars! Tricksters!' roared the angry cat as he struck wildly at the monkeys nearest to him. 'How dare you trick us all? You shall be punished for such a crime!'

The monkeys screamed and scattered in fright. Even in their slightly drunken state they knew they were in great danger, and so they turned and ran. When the other animals saw what had happened they, too, joined in the chase. The monkeys left the long grass and fled up into the highest trees, but the lithe and limber leopard could also climb trees and the monkeys were chased up into the slenderest, topmost branches.

And there they stayed, for no one else could climb so high. To this day, Inkawu prefers the highest branches. The vervet monkeys seldom come down to the ground – just in case Ingwe the leopard catches them, for he still wants to punish them for their trickery.

The cat that walks alone

Leopard

Panthera pardus

The leopard is one of the most beautiful of the big cats. It is the most widely distributed, living in a huge variety of habitats, throughout Africa and Asia, ranging from deserts to rainforests and from coastal dunes to high mountains.

Leopards are solitary, very secretive, and when close to human settlement – even big cities – move around only at night. Because leopards will kill domestic livestock they have been heavily persecuted.

The leopard is a successful species because it is not specialized. It can live on what-ever the habitat has to offer, from small to medium-sized antelope, rodents, hares, dassies (hyraxes), and even birds, monkeys, small carnivores, reptiles, insects and fish.

The leopard is a stalker and pouncer, relying more on a stealthy approach and a short, explosive burst of speed, than the long chase. Although it feels more at home on the ground – on rock outcrops and termite mounds – it will occasionally pounce down on prey from the branches of a tree. Trees also provide a refuge from other large predators, a vantage point from which to spot quarry, and a safe repository for the leopard's kill (from hyaenas, for example).

Khokhoba and the false suitor

A ZULU TALE

nce, in a remote village of Zululand, there was a huge celebration, with great feasting and dancing. The festivities went on for many days and all the young men displayed their prowess and their skills.

The fairest young maiden in the village was called Nkongwe, and she had eyes only for the tallest and the most handsome young man among all the dancers. Nkongwe decided that no other suitor could possibly meet her requirements. But he was a stranger, and so she pleaded with her father and mother to enquire about him.

Her parents approached the stranger and were impressed by his words: 'I come to seek a bride from your many beautiful maidens,' the stranger told them. 'My home is far away, beyond the mountains to the west, but a good bride price awaits the father of the one I choose.'

So they invited him to their kraal and treated him with favours and great respect. The more that Nkongwe saw of the fine young man, the more she fell in love with him and the more insistent she became with her parents that no other suitor – and there were many others – would make her happy. In time, arrangements were made for their wedding celebrations and a most generous *lobola*, or dowry price, was agreed upon.

The wedding took place with a much merrymaking, and Nkongwe and her handsome new husband settled down in her village and were very happy. They tilled the land given them by the chief and planted crops.

When this was completed the young husband suggested that the time had come to celebrate the marriage at his own home with his own family. Nkongwe was delighted with the idea and readily agreed to go with him.

Now Nkongwe had a younger brother called Khokhoba and he was most impressed with his sister's new husband, spending much time with him so as to learn the ways of a warrior and hunter. On the day of their departure the bridegroom said to his wife, 'The day is hot so I will go to the river to bathe and prepare for the journey!'

As Khokhoba was an inquisitive young man, he wanted to ask his brother-in-law about his home and the ways of his people, so he quietly slipped away from the kraal and also made his way down to the river. But Khokhoba was not expecting to see such a horrifying and dismaying sight for, as he hid behind a nearby bush, the stranger carefully slipped out of his soft, gleaming skin to show the rough, hairy body of a huge baboon.

With a gasp of fear Khokhoba ran for home as fast as he could. He went straight to his sister's hut and told her of the dreadful scene he had just witnessed. Nkongwe was sure her little brother was making up this ridiculous story just to prevent her from leaving the kraal and settling far away from her home and family. No matter how often he assured her he was telling the truth, she would not believe that her fine new husband was a wicked baboon in disguise. So, when her husband returned from the river, looking as handsome and distinguished as ever, all was ready and she set off with him with a heart full of joy and great expectations for her new home and family beyond the mountains.

Khokhoba was very fond of his sister and, not wishing any harm to come to her, followed closely behind. When they were a good distance from home he showed himself and begged to be allowed to accompany them on their journey. Neither Nkongwe nor her husband objected to this, and the three young people travelled on together.

It was a long, tiring walk as they penetrated deeper and deeper into the wild and inhospitable bush. And all the while Khokhoba became more and more worried, holding his sister's arm from time to time, trying to persuade her to turn back. But Nkongwe would hear none of it and pulled her arm away impatiently.

On they trudged, eventually reaching a collection of rough and ragged huts that had no doors. All of them were empty.

'Now,' said the bridegroom, 'you must wait for me in this hut while I go to gather my people for the marriage feast.'

When they were safely inside he pushed large rocks across the hut entrance so that they could not get out. Hastily Khokhoba pulled aside some of the grass thatching in time to see the bridegroom quickly slip from his outer, magical skin and set off, in his baboon form, towards the nearby forest. He called his sister and she just glimpsed the huge hairy figure disappearing among a dense stand of trees. Undoubtedly he was going to fetch his troop.

Khokhoba was a strong and resourceful young man and he quickly cut a hole in the roof with his knife. Pulling Nkongwe after him they sped off down a track in the opposite direction to that which the baboon had taken. They soon came to a river that was deep and swiftly flowing, and it barred their way.

Undeterred, the boy once again used his knife to cut the long, hollow reeds that lined the bank of the river. Using strong creepers that were hanging in nearby trees, he tied them together to make a raft. One especially large reed could be used as a pole.

The two runaways heard the sounds of a commotion from the direction of the village, and knew that their escape had been discovered. They threw themselves onto the raft just as a troop of large and fierce baboons burst out of the vegetation. They stood on the banks, screaming their rage.

'Come back, come back to the marriage feast!' cried their wicked leader.

Now Khokhoba and his sister knew something of the ways of baboons, and they quickly contrived a plan.

'Our raft is heavy and we cannot steer it!' replied Khokhoba. 'Plait a rope from the creepers and throw it to us, so that you may pull us back to you!'

But as he said these words, Khokhoba was poling the raft into the middle of the stream, towards where the current was at its strongest. Slowly it responded to his struggle, and by the time the baboons had hastily made a creeper rope, the first strong current caught their flimsy craft.

With a mighty heave, the big baboon flung the rope out to them whilst the rest of the troop held onto the other end of the rope. Knowing what they did, the brother and sister tied their end of the rope to the raft. Now the water was swiftly carrying them downstream.

Their plan worked. Like most monkeys, baboons cannot let go once their hands close on an object they want. So, one by one, the raft in the current pulled the baboons off the bank and into the river, and, one by one, it pulled them under the water and drowned them.

Nkongwe and her resourceful little brother floated away to safety. The river bore them downstream to a stretch of the bank that they recognized and Khokhoba poled them to the shore. They were most relieved to be once again in the safety of their family and village.

To this day baboons have still not learnt to release an object they desire, even if it means putting themselves in danger.

The Zulu

The first of the Nguni groups arrived in what is today KwaZulu-Natal some 500 years ago, a loose confederation of about 800 different clans.

Then Shaka succeeded to the Zulu chieftainship and quickly transformed the circumstances of his people. He expanded and reorganized the army, and introduced new weapons, notably the assegai. He adopted new battle tactics to produce the famous 'ox' formation. Regiments in the field, collectively known as the *impi*, would divide into four groups. The central 'chest' would clash head-on with the enemy; the second and third groups, the 'horns', would deploy in an encircling movement; the fourth would stand ready for the final assault.

The Zulus conquered all neighbouring clans in just a few years, but were in turn confronted by the Voortrekkers, and then by the British, who crushed the Zulu army at Ulundi.

Traditional Zulu clothes were of hides and pelts, adorned by the fighting men to distinguish their regiments. Most spectacular were the plumes and patterned ox-hide shields. Bright beads, introduced by traders, were stitched together in intricate designs, each colour taking on a symbolic meaning.

Zulu ceremonial occasions are vibrant affairs. The main traditional musical instrument is the cowhide drum – and the human voice, which is still used to magnificent effect.

The magic of the little Honeyguide

A SHANGAAN TALE

Once there were two brothers who left their village to hunt in the bush. Each carried a bow and some arrows and a leather bag slung over his shoulder. They hoped to fill the leather bags with food for their family. For a long time they trudged along a sandy trail that led them from their village and out into the wild country, where only a few intrepid travellers and hunters would venture. All they saw was the occasional snake that slithered across their path, the odd guinea fowl, or a francolin that would leap, squawking, into the air from the grass at their feet. The further they went, the more rugged the country became, full of boulders and thick thorn scrub.

Suddenly, they came across a row of red clay pots, all standing upside down.

'What does this mean?' asked the younger brother. 'Who would leave pots in a wild and deserted place such as this?'

'Do not touch them!' said the elder brother in a worried voice. 'I do not like the look of them. I sense that there is magic about them and I think we had better leave them alone.'

But the younger brother, who had always been the braver and more adventurous of the two, refused to pass by.

'I am going to look beneath these pots, no matter what you say,' he said, and he bent down to peer beneath the pots. As he stood them the right way up, his elder brother ran a distance away and then stood and watched anxiously.

At first it seemed there was no magic here after all, but as the younger brother turned over the last pot, out jumped a little old woman. The boy gave a shout of surprise.

The little old woman took no notice of the younger brother, not even to say thank you for releasing her from beneath the pot! Instead she shouted at the elder brother, 'Do not stand there shivering like a frightened buck. Follow me and I will show you a sight worth seeing.'

But the boy was terrified and would not take even one pace towards her.

'Coward!' she shouted after him again. Now she turned to the younger brother and commanded him to follow her. He was always keen for adventure and eagerly followed the little old woman. He followed her for quite a distance until, suddenly, she came to a halt in front of an enormous old tree. She then handed the boy an axe and said, 'Cut this tree down for me!'

As the first stroke cut into the tree, out stepped a bullock. With the next stroke a cow, then a goat, then a sheep. With each stroke of the axe, an animal appeared and soon a huge herd of livestock and flocks of fowls surrounded him.

'These are for you!' said the woman. 'You must now drive them back to your home. I shall stay here.'

The boy was too amazed to speak, but eventually he recovered enough to thank the little old woman in the proper manner. He drove the animals in front of him, and soon he came to the place where he had left his more timid elder brother waiting.

'Just look what the old woman gave me!' exclaimed the jubilant boy. 'Do you not wish you had followed her as she asked you to?'

He then told his brother all that had happened, and together they began to drive the flocks and herds back towards their village.

As it was the middle of the dry season, the land was scorched and brown and it was not long before the boys became very thirsty. The animals cried loudly as they too were thirsty, and the land offered little for them to eat. Further on they came to a precipice and the elder brother looked carefully over the edge.

Suddenly the elder brother shouted, 'Look! Water!' Down there, far below them, was the sparkle of a stream wandering through the trees. 'If you tie a rope to me, you can lower me down so that I can drink my fill!'

The younger brother did as he was asked, and as soon as the elder brother had finished his drink, he hauled him up, refreshed and cheerful.

'Now let me down on the rope,' said the younger brother, and the elder brother let out the rope so that his brother could quench his thirst as well. But now an evil thought came to the elder boy. He knew that there was no way to climb up from the valley and so he threw the rope over the edge, and turned around and continued to drive the animals back to his village. The younger brother was left at the foot of the precipice to perish.

The journey home was long and tedious and, when he arrived, his parents greeted the elder brother with surprise. They had not expected their sons back so soon and certainly not one without the other. When they questioned him, he lied to his parents.

'An old woman gave these animals to me!' he said.

'But where is your brother?' they asked him, with great consternation.

'Has he not returned? He grew tired of our journey and he left, saying he would come home. I have not seen him since midday,' replied the boy deceitfully.

Naturally the younger brother did not come home that night, but the parents were not too concerned, thinking that he might have changed his mind and gone hunting elsewhere. He was, after all, the adventurous one.

Early the following morning the women of the village went to gather water for the day from the nearby stream. Here they heard the song of the helpful honeyguide, a bird who leads people to beehives with his song, always hoping for some delicious scraps of leftover comb. Delighted, the mother of the two boys ran back to her husband and told him to follow the bird and gather some fresh honey for them. So the husband, together with several other men from the village, set off to follow the honeyguide.

Every so often, the honeyguide would pause and sing to allow the humans to catch up with it, and then it would fly on, deeper and ever deeper into the desolate bush. The men followed the bird so far that, after a while, they scarcely knew where they were.

Eventually one of them called to the others, 'I have gone far enough! This bird is not leading us to honey. I am becoming very weary, so I think I will stop following it now and return home!'

At this the bird began to sing and chirp even louder. It grew so frantic that it puzzled the men.

The father of the two boys said, 'It would almost seem as if the bird is trying to tell us something. Let us follow it a little further.'

So on they went, and eventually they reached the precipice. Far below them they could hear the faint voice of someone calling for help. The honeyguide flew to and fro excitedly and then swooped down into the valley – and landed at the boy's feet.

The father leant out, over the edge, straining to see where the bird had gone.

'My son!' he exclaimed. 'I believe I can hear my son!'

Quickly the men fashioned a rope from some lianas nearby and very soon they had hauled the younger brother out from the chasm. He told them all of his adventures.

'Alas!' wept the father, 'that I should have a son as wicked as your elder brother. You would have perished had it not been for the magic of the honeyguide that led us here.'

'The other boy must be punished,' the men agreed angrily. 'It was only greed that made him leave his brother here in the valley, and to pretend that the cattle were his own.'

News of the younger son's rescue must have reached the village before the men returned, as the elder brother was nowhere to be found. He had vanished, never to be seen again. But the younger brother prospered as his herds and flocks increased, and his parents wanted for nothing in their old age.

Unlikely partners in crime

Greater Honeyguide
Indicator indicator

The Greater Honeyguide does just what its name suggests – it guides people (and animals such as baboons and honey badgers) to beehives. This behaviour has probably developed over some two million years, from the time when our distant ancestors first walked upright, or at least when they discovered fire.

This is called a symbiotic relationship, where two completely different life forms work together for the benefit of both. Here, the human is led to the beehive and takes most of the honey. To do so, he must drive away the bees (usually with fire) and destroy their hive – too tough a job for the honeyguide. The bird, in turn, can feast on the scattered bits and pieces that are left over.

This drab little brown bird could be overlooked were it not for the fuss it makes when it has located a hive and sets about attracting attention. In fact, honey-gatherers can summon a honey-guide simply by hitting an axe against a tree a few times.

When they find you, they chatter non-stop with a rasping 'churr' (the sound can be imitated by rattling a half-empty box of matches) and flit from tree to tree in the direction of the hive. When they perch, they fan their tails to make their white outer tail feathers serve as a beacon, or indicator (hence their scientific name).

It is customary to leave a piece of honeycomb or a bee grub or two for the bird as a reward for its help – and to make sure it is willing to help you find honey again.

The Shangaan

The Shangaan are believed to have originated in the West African rainforests thousands of years ago, and then migrated eastwards and southwards, eventually settling in what is now the KwaZulu-Natal Province in South Africa.

Here they lived in relative peace until the young Zulu chief Shaka came to power in the early 1800s, and with his powerful army, new military tactics and a new strategy, swiftly overcame the neighbouring clans. The Shangaan group resisted stoutly; however, after several bloody conflicts, the Shangaan *impis* were defeated and Shoshangana, their chief, fled together with his people to the north. Today they live in a region that spreads across the borders of Mozambique, Zimbabwe, and South Africa.

The Shangaan have largely retained their culture. Some distinctive customs include piercing the earlobes and cutting and tatooing the face. Rural communties keep cattle, till the soil and are expert fishermen. The Shangaan have a rich folklore and excel in telling stories, of which around 200, together with 1 900 proverbs, have been recorded. Traditionally they believe in a Supreme Being, *Tilo* ('heaven'), and in the presence of ancestral spirits, but there is no actual ancestor-worship.

Why the Reed Warbler babbles

A SHONA TALE

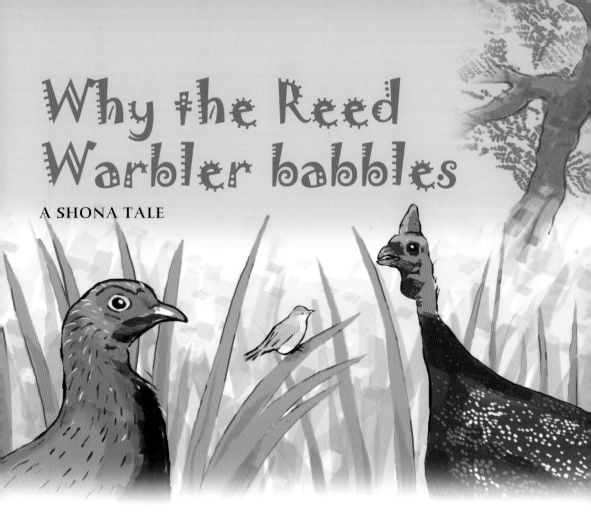

This old fable from the Ndawu clan tells us why the tiny little reed warbler always makes so much noise. It begins in the days, long ago, when all the birds of the Earth wore white feathers only.

One day, a dozen or so birds gathered beside the water hole and were talking about this and that, but mostly about the dangers in their lives.

'I am so lucky to be alive!' said the francolin. 'If I had not been able to run so fast and if the grass had not been so thick, that hunter would have had me as sure as ants are ants. As it is, one of his arrows took a feather out of my tail.'

The francolin was understandably very upset, for it had been a most alarming experience. And it was not as if it had been an isolated incident, though it was the first time it had been so close as to cost a tail feather. The guinea fowl had a similar story to tell, and so had the quail, and on many an occasion the snipe had had to dodge the hunter's arrow at the last moment.

'Is there nothing that we can do to protect ourselves?' they asked each other. But not one of them could come up with a solution.

'Cheer up! Cheer up! Do not look so glum!' said the little reed warbler as he ran down the stem of a flowering reed that grew beside the water hole. 'No one should look so glum. I never do.'

'I do not like anyone to look glum or be sad and unhappy either,' chirped the sunbird as he flitted from flower to flower in his search for nectar. 'No one should be unhappy on a wonderful day such as today, when the sun is shining brightly and the flowers are beautiful and gay!'

'You would not be so cheerful if you had our troubles!' replied the snipe.

'We have our troubles too,' the reed warbler interrupted, 'but some of us do not make such a fuss about it. I think the sunbird is absolutely right and I think the flowers are very beautiful and colourful and gay!' He babbled on in his usual way, but no one paid him any attention. They all knew that the reed warbler's chatter never ceased.

'You know,' said the sunbird suddenly, 'I think it is a pity that the birds are not coloured like the flowers. It is rather dull to be just white – all of us just white. It would be much more fun if I were blue and you were green and the francolin red!'

'I should like to be red. No, purple. Or maybe yellow. I wonder what would suit me best? It is so difficult to decide. Maybe even a mix of colours … like the rainbow!' The little reed warbler was off again, rambling to himself rather than to his audience.

'If we were green, or perhaps a dusty brown, we would find it much easier to hide from the hunter,' said the snipe slowly, as though thinking out aloud.

'Then if we were to lie quite still, it would be far more difficult for our enemies to see us.'

'Yes, yes!' the francolin and quail agreed with enthusiasm. 'They would never see us if we were the colour of the earth and grass.'

'I like being white!' said the egret.

'Oh no! Colours would be much nicer,' several birds spoke up in unison, and as dozens more arrived the gathering became a clamorous affair, all the birds joining in with their opinions. At length the fish eagle came to see what all the noise was about. As he landed on a thorn tree near the water hole and folded his huge wings, the chattering ceased for just a moment.

Then the reed warbler's voice could be heard piping up. 'Look, there is the fish eagle,' he said. 'I wonder what colour he thinks would suit me best. Shall I go and ask him?'

'No! And stop going on so much,' said the snipe, who, like most of the other birds, was getting tired of the reed warbler's never-ending vanity.

It was the sunbird who flew up to the fish eagle and described the wonderful idea that the birds had come up with. But, of course, it was only a wish, not a proper plan.

So the sunbird asked the wise eagle how they could arrange to be as colourful and beautiful as the flowers. The fish eagle pondered over this dilemma for some time and, after long and deliberate thought on the matter, he said: 'This is a very good idea! If all the birds are agreed, I will fly up to the heavens and speak to Lesa, the Great Spirit, and ask if He will give us the gift of colour and make us as beautiful as the flowers. I will ask if this can be done.'

'Yes! Yes!' trilled the reed warbler. 'That is just what we want. Please ask Him if I can be the first to be coloured and tell Him that I want to be red and purple and …'

His little voice was soon shouted down by the gathering of birds, 'Yes, yes!' they cried, 'we all want to be as colourful as the flowers!'

'I like being white,' muttered the egret balefully, but nobody paid any attention to his wishes.

'Very well, I shall go to Lesa and request this favour.' So the fish eagle spread his mighty wings and soared off into the heavens.

Lesa agreed to the request, and on the appointed day all the birds gathered before His throne. The throne was set about by dozens of huge pots full of all the coloured dyes that you can think of.

'Me first! Me first! Do me first!' chirped the reed warbler. 'Do me first!'

All the other birds stood or perched around quietly, all patiently waiting their turn. All, that is, except for the reed warbler. He just hopped up and down, chirping impatiently, 'My turn first, do me now!'

But because it had been his idea, the sunbird went first and was painted as he requested. Lesa transformed him into a living jewel. Flashing, now green, now red, now yellow, he darted to and fro. His head, neck, throat and back gleamed in a miracle of iridescent metallic hues and, as he flew around, all the other birds marvelled at his beauty, a beauty that could match that of any flower.

'I want to be just like the sunbird, I want to be painted all the colours of the rainbow! I want to be painted next!' the reed warbler continued chirping, on and on and on …

But next Lesa painted the oriole in shades of yellow and gold, and then the pigeon green and then gave the purple-crested lourie his coat of blue and green with vivid crimson wings.

'Me next! Me next! Do me now!' the reed warbler chirped, to everyone's annoyance. He hopped up and down, but Lesa took no notice of him and 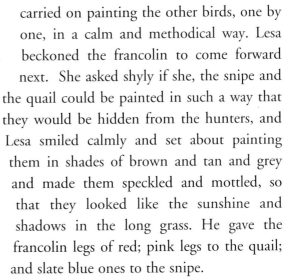 carried on painting the other birds, one by one, in a calm and methodical way. Lesa beckoned the francolin to come forward next. She asked shyly if she, the snipe and the quail could be painted in such a way that they would be hidden from the hunters, and Lesa smiled calmly and set about painting them in shades of brown and tan and grey and made them speckled and mottled, so that they looked like the sunshine and shadows in the long grass. He gave the francolin legs of red; pink legs to the quail; and slate blue ones to the snipe.

'Me next! Me next!' broke in the annoying little reed warbler, and impatiently hopped up onto one of the pots of paint that stood next to the throne.

'You shall have your wish,' Lesa at last agreed, with a frown on His face. And He quickly painted the little bird and then told him to fly away. He then beckoned to the egret.

'You are a really beautiful white bird,' Lesa said. 'Do you wish to be changed?'

'No!' said the egret. 'I am proud of my whiteness. I like being white and have no wish to change and look like the others. Please let me stay as I am.'

'And so you shall,' said Lesa, and beckoned the roller to come forth.

'Look at me! Look at me!' sang the reed warbler triumphantly. 'I am more beautiful than the sunbird. I am more stunning than the oriole. I am more handsome than the lourie. Look at me! Look at me!'

'Oh, be quiet!' scolded the other birds, and they watched intently as Lesa transformed the roller, giving him lilac breast feathers and wings and tail feathers the deep blue of an eastern sky at twilight. Lesa painted his head a rich coppery brown. Even a bit of emerald green flecked his head and wings.

'Oh! How beautiful!' the birds murmured in admiration.

'I am just as beautiful,' chirped the reed warbler, as he waddled up and down to show himself off. 'Look at me, I am just as beautiful as the roller. Am I not?' he added as, suddenly, doubt came over him. 'What colour am I, by the way? Blue? Green? Red?'

'No!' said the snipe curtly.

'Well what colour am I?' asked the reed warbler with a worried tone in his squeaky little voice.

'Just brown! Plain old brown!'

'What!' shrieked the reed warbler. 'Not coloured? Not like the rainbow? Not like a beautiful little flower? Not even red or purple?' The warbler could not believe he was just brown!

'Quiet!' commanded Lesa. 'You make far too much noise for one so small! I would have given you all the colours you may have wished for, but you were too rude and impatient. Try to learn patience like the others, little warbler.'

Ashamed, the reed warbler hung his head whilst Lesa took a humble little starling in His hand and painted him a glowing sapphire blue.

And so, to this day the reed warbler is a drab little brown bird, easy to overlook in the reed beds by the rivers and pans of Africa – easy to overlook, that is, if it were not for the shrill and constant noise he makes. In his ceaseless babbling, no doubt, he is complaining of the way he missed out on being as beautiful as the flowers.

The golden citadel

The Great Zimbabwe Ruins

Some thousand years ago, the Karanga people, ancestors of the modern Shona in Zimbabwe, built a city, known as Great Zimbabwe, the largest stone structure to have been built in Africa south of the Sahara.

The highly organized society that established this citadel was based on cultivation, livestock husbandry and gold mining. It was the centre of a vast, wealthy empire that stretched across much of modern-day Zimbabwe, trading with the Arabs, and later the Portuguese, on the eastern coast. But the empire was doomed by its own success: its population grew, and its resources became depleted. By the year 1500 the citadel was deserted, its great walls and stone enclosures lying silent in the hot sun.

Hare and the King of the Beasts

A SOTHO TALE

The elders tell us that in the earliest of times Lion, the King of the Beasts, was the most feared of all creatures, and that his hunting skills were extraordinary.

So many animals were being eaten by the King that all the creatures of the wild called a special council to see how they could be saved from extinction.

Eventually, they decided they should go to the lion and suggest a compromise – an offer to sacrifice a few for the safety of them all.

When asked if he would agree to eat only one animal a day and leave the rest alone, the lion pondered on this offer at length. Eventually he nodded.

So the animals drew lots each day, and it was the task of the loser to present himself or herself to the lion to be devoured. The first day the steenbok was the loser. Bravely she walked to the lion's den and he pounced on her and ate at his leisure. Next day, it was the turn of the impala, then the kudu, and then the reedbuck, and so it went on day after day.

Eventually, it fell to the lot of the hare to be the next victim, and the other animals prepared to drag him, kicking and screaming, to the lion's den.

But Hare told them he was prepared to meet his fate, and that he could walk there calmly. There was no need for any undignified dragging. But the hare did not go directly to the lion. First he went home and slept till noon.

By then the lion was hungry and most displeased that his meal had not arrived in the agreed way. So he set off through the bush, roaring his displeasure as he went. Eventually he found Hare, who had climbed up a tree that overlooked a deep well.

As the lion drew near, Hare shouted down to him, 'What are you making all that dreadful noise for?'

The lion replied that his daily meal had not arrived, but that he was searching for it, and that he was very angry that it had not arrived as he had agreed with the animals. He was beginning to wonder if he should start hunting again, to remind them who really was the King of the Beasts.

'Well I was chosen by the lot to be your meal for the day,' replied the hare. 'And I had brought you a present of honey as well. But I met another lion and he took the honey from me!'

'Where is this other lion?' roared the King furiously.

'He is in the well,' said Hare, 'but he is not afraid of you and says that he is bigger and stronger than you.'

Now that really made the lion angrier than ever, and he went straight over to the well. He peered down and saw another lion looking up at him, and he

too looked angry. The King of the Beasts shouted insults at the intruder, but silence was his only reply. The lion then resorted to shouting every insult and slander at the impostor, even insulting his parents, but to no response. This incensed the King so much that he could no longer control his rage. He leapt down into the well and on top of the other lion.

Too late did he realize his foolishness, for it was only his reflection that greeted him before he splashed into a watery grave.

And that was how Hare tricked the King of Beasts, and saved the animals of the bush.

Hare, the legendary trickster

Scrub Hare
Lepus saxatilis

Throughout Africa the hare is the star of fable and legend. He is depicted as a trickster who is always quick to pull a prank on the other characters of the bush. He is especially fond of making the high and mighty look stupid and silly and he will invariably, in any situation, come out on top. Hare is so entrenched in folklore that he was taken to the Americas with Africans abducted into slavery. Here he become the legendary 'Brer Rabbit', who was usually pitted against the wily old fox. In African regions where the hare does not occur, such as the equatorial rainforests, Hare has often been replaced by the spider as the trickster character.

The scrub hare is the larger of the two species of hare that occur in southern Africa and is the more widespread. But there's one unusual thing about its distribution – the hare gets smaller the further north one goes. The southwestern variety weighs about 3 kilograms and measures 144 millimetres while a hare from Zimbabwe weighs 2 kilograms and measures 97 millimetres.

The hare is solitary. During the day it lies up in a form (a hollow in the ground) and comes out at night to feed on grass, leaves, stems and rhizomes. While it is resting, it keeps its ears folded down. When a hare is approached, it will freeze to avoid detection, but if the approach is too close it will bolt for thicker cover with an explosive dash.

The Sotho

The BaSotho are part of a group of more than 50 separate peoples who arrived in southern Africa over 600 years ago. They followed a largely cattle-herding way of life and were renowned for their skills in working iron and in weaving (notably baskets).

The BaSotho prospered and grew in strength until the early 1800s, when the advancing *impis* of the Zulu king, Shaka, launched an era of conflict. One Sotho clan leader called Moshweshwe led his people into the high Maloti (or Drakensberg) range and found safe haven at Thaba Bosiu, which means 'Mountain of the Night'. By the time of his death Moshweshwe had built a strong, well-organized society in this mountain refuge, one that had been able to beat back all attempts to conquer it.

Traditionally, the BaSotho have a strong affinity with the spirit world. Recognition of the presence and power of the ancestors is essential to ensure the wellbeing of the living. Witchdoctors, or *Ngaka*, are powerful people, second only to the chief in importance, able to interpret the signs from the spirit world and thus to guard the community against misfortune and evil.

In the early days, when the BaSotho were trying to escape the power of the Zulu, life was extremely harsh, and many clans were forced to resort to raiding their neighbours, and to eating their crops and livestock.

The magic verandah pole

A VENDA TALE

nce upon a time, there lived a young man whose mother and father had died. He lived all alone, spending his days herding cattle in the lonely bush, returning each evening to his empty, ramshackle hut with nothing but the cold, moaning night wind to keep him company.

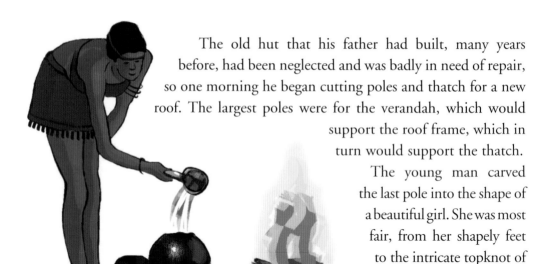

The old hut that his father had built, many years before, had been neglected and was badly in need of repair, so one morning he began cutting poles and thatch for a new roof. The largest poles were for the verandah, which would support the roof frame, which in turn would support the thatch.

The young man carved the last pole into the shape of a beautiful girl. She was most fair, from her shapely feet to the intricate topknot of hair that helped support the thatch edge. The few people who passed by would remark on how fine the carving was. The young man in his loneliness would often talk to the verandah pole as he went about his household tasks.

One day, soon after the young man had left for the bush with his herd of cattle, the pole stirred, shook itself, and turned into a human form – into a beautiful young girl.

The lovely girl then swept the courtyard, smeared the floor with fresh cow dung, and finally put porridge and water in pots next to the fire, ready to be cooked. When the young man returned from the bush, he was astonished to find his household chores had been completed. He had no idea who could have done this for him, for the girl had turned back into the verandah pole.

Many times this happened until, one day, the young man was determined to solve this mystery. So, instead of herding his cattle as he usually did, he hid himself in a clump of ferns near the path to the hut. He watched the hut, and was amazed to see the pole turn into a beautiful girl – the work of his own hands had become a living, breathing being. He leapt forth from the ferns and clasped her by the hands. He declared his love for her, and expressed his wish to marry her. She gladly accepted his offer, and the two lived together in bliss and contentment. Never again, she said, would she be a lifeless piece of wood.

Some time later, a messenger from the chief arrived to say that all the people must come together to work at the chief's kraal.

'You must come,' the messenger commanded the young man. 'And bring your wife too. Not one person can remain behind. Whoever lingers will be subject to a heavy fine!'

The young man had a strong feeling of foreboding and said, 'But I have no wife! I will come alone.'

'You're lying!' replied the messenger. 'You have a wife. If you leave her behind you will pay a large fine!'

The young man's fears were soon realized. The chief had an eye for beauty, and as soon as he saw the young bride, he knew that he wanted her as his junior wife. 'She must not work out in the hot sun,' the chief said. 'Let's put her to work in the shade with the bearers of food.' The young man's party finished early and departed for home. The bride's party worked until sunset, however, and when they had finished and began leaving, the chief kept the beautiful young woman behind and took her in as his junior wife.

While the young man's party was making its way slowly back home, the other work party came singing cheerfully through the bush in the twilight. As the women drew level with them, the young man saw that his bride was not among them.

'Where is my wife?' he asked.

They all stopped singing and looked sad as they replied, 'She is not with us. The chief has taken her as his junior wife!'

The young man was distraught, but he did not know what he could do. Loneliness once again enveloped him, and now it seemed ten times worse than before, since now he knew how sweet companionship could be.

So he resolved to get his wife back, even if he should die in the attempt.

Taking his musical bow and gourd, he returned to the chief's kraal, but this time in the guise of a wandering minstrel. At the meeting place he played his instrument and danced and sang. The words of his song were so haunting that people stopped to listen; some called for the chief's wives to come and hear the melancholy stranger. When he saw his wife standing with the chief's other wives, he sang his sweetest melodies and, as she listened, tears welled up in her eyes. Suddenly, a dust devil whirled through the kraal. When it cleared, the chief's junior wife was nowhere to be seen. All that remained in the meeting place was a carved verandah pole, lying on the ground.

The lonely young man went back to his remote hut in the bush while the people gathered around the pole in amazement.

'How odd is this?' they asked each other. 'We must tell the chief of these strange happenings!'

When he saw what had become of his junior wife, the chief was afraid.

'The singer must be a powerful *nganga*. I want no part in sorcery!' he said. 'Take this pole and return it to his home, for it is of no value to me.'

So the people of the royal kraal returned the verandah pole to the young man's hut and they threw it to the ground at the entrance.

'Here is your verandah pole!' they called out. 'Our chief has no use for it!'

As soon as the people had left, the pole changed back into the beautiful young girl, and the couple embraced in great joy. The chief was afraid of the young man, who he believed possessed great magical powers – and so the young couple were left in peace to live a happy and contented life.

The Venda

The BaVenda originated in the far north and it is believed that they migrated south into the beautiful Soutspansberg range of mountains, whose slopes and valleys are well watered and fertile. The lofty peaks and many watercourses were a relief from the fever-ridden Lowveld areas they had travelled through, and they named their new home Venda, which means 'the pleasant land'.

The many caves and shelters of the area had been home to the Bushmen (or San), whom the BaVenda drove out into the harshness of the dry lands to the west. The BaVenda say the forests still rustle and whisper with the unhappy voices of the Bushman ancestors and, no matter how weary, a traveller is strongly advised not to rest in the shade of the trees.

The Python God is the most powerful deity of the BaVenda. The ancestral spirits also have great influence in daily life. One ritual that persists from ancient times is the Python Dance, or *Domba*, performed by anything between 20 and 200 young girls as part of their initiation into womanhood. The undulations of the long line of youngsters mimic those of the sinuous serpent.

The crafty Jackal and the proud Hyaena

A XHOSA TALE

Jackal and Hyaena were once neighbours. Hyaena did not bother himself much with the affairs of Jackal, but Jackal made it his business to learn about all the doings that were the concern of Hyaena.

One day the hyaena went to the kraal of a nearby chief and proposed marriage to the chief's daughter. He postured and strode about speaking of his strength, his bravery and his powers of endurance. Hyaena praised himself so much that the chief's daughter thought him a very fine person indeed. She accepted his overtures and agreed to become betrothed to him.

Hyaena was very proud of this. At first he intended to keep the whole affair a secret, but in his pride he could not help mentioning it to his closest friends in the strictest of confidence. So, naturally, the betrothal became known to Jackal, whose ears were always wide open for the gossip of the neighbourhood.

Jackal was jealous of the hyaena. So he planned a way to spoil the hyaena's prospects. He went to visit the chief's daughter and also proposed to her. She told him that she was unable to accept his offer as she was already betrothed to Hyaena.

At this the jackal feigned surprise and exclaimed, 'I can scarcely believe that! Do you mean to say you are really betrothed to that hyaena! How did you come to accept the attention of such a common person?'

The girl said, 'The hyaena is big and strong and brave, and seems to me to be a fine fellow!'

Jackal asked, 'Who told you these fantastical things about him?'

The girl replied, 'Why! The hyaena himself told me!'

Jackal scoffed, 'Hyaena has a fat stomach, and the hair on it is so long that it trails along the ground. One day that hair of his will catch fire, then he will set the whole countryside alight and you will be a widow.' He kept on pressing his offers of marriage, but each time the girl repeated that she could not marry him, as she was already betrothed to the hyaena.

Jackal said, 'You should marry a person who is your equal. As for Hyaena, he is my servant – I ride him as if he were a donkey. One day I will show you that this is so!'

And Jackal then went on his way. As he was trotting along, he met the hyaena and asked him if he had any news. Hyaena said that there was indeed exciting news and that there was soon to be a great wedding with a big feast. Jackal pretended not to know of these events and asked whose wedding it might be. Hyaena could not contain his pride, 'Why it is my own wedding. I am betrothed to the daughter of the chief.'

Jackal said he was very pleased to hear such good news, and asked whether he might act as Hyaena's attendant the next time he went to the kraal to visit the chief's daughter. Hyaena thought that it would be a good idea to visit the chief's kraal with someone in attendance, so he gladly accepted Jackal's offer.

On the arranged day they met again. Jackal had borrowed a *mootsha*, a type of dressed hide apron, and a *sjambok*, a tough hide whip. When Hyaena saw these he asked the jackal why he was wearing a *mootsha* and carrying a *sjambok*. Jackal replied that it was only proper for someone attending to an important person to appear wearing a *mootsha*. As for the *sjambok*, he carried that so he could keep order among the throng of people that were bound to gather as soon as the news of the betrothal became common knowledge. Hyaena was satisfied with this explanation. In fact, he was very pleased with it, as it made him feel even prouder of his good fortune.

So the two of them set off, Hyaena walking in front and Jackal behind, wearing the *mootsha* and carrying the *sjambok* over his shoulder.

After they had travelled some distance, Jackal began to lag behind, so Hyaena called out, 'Hey! Get closer; we are near to the chief's kraal.'

Jackal replied, whining, 'I did not know that the chief's kraal was so far. I am very tired. Also, my foot has been injured and it pains me greatly!'

Hyaena waited as the jackal slowly limped up to him. The *sjambok* was no longer over his shoulder, but trailed behind him. 'I am so utterly exhausted,' Jackal complained. 'I can go no further unless you, Hyaena, who are renowned for your strength and endurance, can carry me.'

But Hyaena shook his hairy head. It was unseemly, he felt, to be seen carrying his own attendant. But Jackal persisted. 'If a great person, such as yourself, cannot carry a little thing like me,' he said, 'then where is your strength? The people at the kraal know that you are strong and brave, and when they ask you, "Where is your attendant?" what will you say if you are unable to carry me? Just tell me and I will lie here under this bush. If I am to die here, then so I shall, but remember, Hyaena, that I set out with you so that you, with an attendant at your heels, might make an impressive show at the kraal of the chief. If weakness has overtaken you, then pass on and be happy. As for me, I am weary and near to death.'

Hyaena regarded the jackal closely. Jackal then drew up his foot as though in great agony. He gasped and panted and moaned, pretending to be utterly exhausted.

Hyaena still eyed him, then said, 'Well, Jackal, if you are unable to go on without help, I will carry you. It will, as you say, be unbecoming for me to arrive at the kraal of the chief without an attendant. So get on my back. But when we approach the place of the chief you must then walk.'

Jackal thanked Hyaena for his kind assistance. He drew himself up, in a show of feigned pain, and with much ado mounted the hyaena's back, placing the *mootsha* under him as one would place a riding blanket. And so they proceeded for a while, at a nice, slow, steady pace.

The jackal said, 'Hyaena, we shall never reach the place of the chief in time for your betrothal ceremony unless you start to trot!' He waved his *sjambok* in the air.

After they had trotted for much of the way to the kraal, Jackal said, 'Hyaena, we are approaching the place of the chief. You should now gallop. This will show everyone at the kraal that, even with a burden, you still move with speed and grace.'

Jackal sat on the hyaena's back and waved the *sjambok* in the air, urging him to even greater speed. Suddenly, he struck his steed a heavy blow on his flanks with the *sjambok*.

'What are you doing?' yelped the hyaena in considerable pain. 'Why do you strike me?'

But Jackal merely said, 'Be quiet. We are very close to the chief's place, where the people will know of your incredible strength and fortitude. When I strike you, show the people that the pain of such a blow is nothing to you.'

So, as they approached the home of the chief, Jackal lashed Hyaena with blow after blow with the cruel *sjambok*.

With each whack, the hyaena ran faster and faster, right to the place where the people had assembled. As they got there, Jackal walloped Hyaena especially hard and then nimbly sprang off his back, saying, 'Go now and eat grass, my steed!'

At this, all the people assembled there laughed loudly and Hyaena, afraid of their ridicule, realized that Jackal had played a devious trick on him. He slunk off into the bush, never to mix in the company of people ever again. The humiliated hyaena was to remain forever slinking around the fringes of human dwellings.

The supreme carnivore

Spotted Hyaena
Crocutta crocutta

The spotted hyaena has long been perceived as a cowardly scavenger, a creature of the night with secretive ways and a sinister laugh. However, it is Africa's most successful large carnivore – a formidable hunter, with immensely powerful jaws.

It has a widely varied diet, and works together with other clan members to tackle and subdue prey as large, strong and dangerous as buffalo, eland and gemsbok. In a group, hyaenas are capable of forcing lions off their kills. They will eat all sorts of carrion, which they locate with their excellent sense of smell. They have good hearing, too, and communicate with other clan members over great distances with their distinctive whooping call. They may look ungainly, but can run at speeds of up to 60 kilometres an hour for up to 3 kilometres, and cover up to 70 kilometres in a single night.

Patrolling members of the clan mark their territory with a secretion from the anal gland. This paste was known as 'hyaena butter', and, according to superstition, was the dripping from the torches of witches that rode on its back. The hyaena's nervous, spooky laugh was believed to be the sound of witches' incantations.

The females are larger, stronger and more dominant than the males. In a communal den, each female digs her own tunnel, or enlarges an old aardvark hole. Here she gives birth to two young, the older one often killing its smaller sibling. Male offspring leave the clan to establish themselves in a new group. Females remain in their mother's clan and often inherit their mother's dominant position.

The Xhosa

The Xhosa, or the 'Red Blanket People' as they are sometimes called, moved down the east coast of Africa over a thousand years ago, settling in the coastal region between the Kiskamma and Bashee Rivers in what is today South Africa's Eastern Cape Province.

The Xhosa fiercely resisted the aggression of both the Zulu and eastward-moving white settlers. But they were eventually defeated – from within. In 1856 a young girl, Nonqawuse, had a vision in which the ancestors commanded the destruction of all cattle and grain. Through her uncle Mhlakaza, a spirit medium, she predicted that after such 'cleansing' the fields would again be ready for reaping, illness and old age would disappear, and the wind would drive the white settlers into the sea. The destruction proved disastrous, leading to mass starvation, a steep decline in the population, and to the end of the Xhosa as a military power.

A Xhosa clan is made up of groups, each led by a chief, or *Inkosi*, who owes his position to his mother's status. In traditional belief, there is a Supreme Being known as *Qwamata* or *Tixo*, and the ancestral spirits are both present and powerful. Misfortune and sickness are attributed to supernatural influences, such as the hairy goblin known as a *tokoloshe*, who might be an instrument of evil if captured by a sorcerer. There are also the huge lightning bird *impundulu* and the gentle *aBantu bomlambo*, human-like beings who are believed to live in rivers and in the sea, and who accept into their family people who drown.

The Xhosa have been known for the splendour and variety of their beadwork, clothes and headdresses.

Jabulani and the Lion

A SWAZI TALE

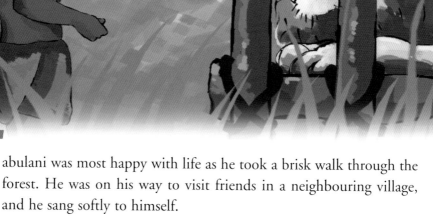

Jabulani was most happy with life as he took a brisk walk through the forest. He was on his way to visit friends in a neighbouring village, and he sang softly to himself.

As he approached a huge log trap that one of the local hunters had built, a pitiful voice wavered up to him, 'Jabulani, my dear friend, please release me from this trap, as I am dying from thirst and hunger!'

Now Jabulani was kind at heart and was always ready to help those in need. But in this case the plea came from a starving lion trapped in the cage. 'If I release you, you will no doubt satisfy your hunger by eating me!' answered the young man.

'Oh no! I promise most faithfully that I will not eat you. Please have pity on me and set me free!' pleaded the poor creature.

'Well,' said the kind-hearted boy, 'if I have your solemn promise, I will help you.' So Jabulani lifted the heavy logs that made the door of the trap. It was the kind that had bait inside, with a trip string that springs the trapdoor closed.

The lion backed out immediately and stretched his cramped limbs and said, 'I must first go to the river so that I may slake my thirst, and then I will return and eat you!'

'Oh! But you forget your promise,' the frightened youth reminded the lion.

'What is a promise when you are as hungry as I?' snarled the lion, revealing his long yellow fangs.

'But please,' begged Jabulani, 'let us ask your fellow creatures if it is correct that you should go back on your word in such a manner. Let them decide.'

'Very well,' agreed the lion, and the two of them walked towards the river so that the lion might quench his thirst. On the way they met a sad old donkey.

'Friend,' said the boy, 'please give your judgment between my lord the lion and me. I found him securely caught in a strong trap and he begged me to free him, promising that if I did so, he would not eat me. So I set him free and now he says he will eat me! Is this justice?'

The donkey pondered the question for some time before replying, 'Yes, it is fair that he should eat you, for you humans have no pity on us animals. When I was young and useful to my master, he cared for me, and I cheerfully carried his loads on my back. He gave me good food, and treated me with kindness. But now that I am too old to work, he has driven me from the comfort of the only home I have known, to die of starvation, for my teeth are too worn to pull on the tough winter grass. Does treatment such as this deserve consideration? I agree with my lord lion, that he should eat you!'

'But this is only the opinion of one animal,' the boy pointed out. 'To be really fair we must ask them all.' Again the lion agreed, but this time more grudgingly.

The next animal they met was the cow, and Jabulani told her the same story that he had told the donkey. The cow shook her head angrily, 'Ha! Humans!' she said. 'You are all the same. When we are young we are among your most cherished belongings. We give you our milk willingly in return for nourishment, and we pull your plows to grow your crops. But when our useful years are over, what happens? You kill us and eat us! You use our hides to clothe your bodies. It is surely justice that you should provide a meal. I agree with my lord, the lion. It is right that he should eat you.' The cow pawed the ground with her hoof to emphasize her displeasure.

'But there are others, especially the wild creatures,' said the boy, who was now badly frightened. 'There are many more animals, and we have heard the opinion of only two. You did agree that we should ask them all.'

'Oh, well,' complained the lion, 'as you wish, but hurry, for my hunger grows, and there is little doubt that the replies will all be the same.' As the lion said this they met a second lion, to whom Jabulani repeated his story.

'Now listen, human,' snarled the second lion. 'Day by day, my life is in danger from your kind. I cannot stop at the water's edge to quench my thirst without forever looking over my shoulder in fear that a spear or arrow may be hurtling towards me from some crafty hunter waiting in ambush. Can we live in peace, with such dangers dogging our every footstep from your kind? No! It is surely right that my brother should eat you!'

'But please, good friend – and remember you also called me "friend" before I released you from the trap – let us ask the antelopes,' begged the now petrified boy, 'for they, too, are creatures of the wild.'

But the first antelope they met also condemned the human race.

'We live in fear all of our lives,' the sable said, ' because of your hunters and their dogs, whose one and only desire is to kill and eat us, just to ease *their* hunger. Is it not right that now you, too, should provide a meal for one of our kind who is hungry?'

Jabulani was giving up hope of ever seeing his home and family again. But then he remembered that the crafty jackal was least likely to condemn humans for, even though they persecuted him just like the other animals, he was able to prosper and multiply thanks to their wastefulness and carelessness.

Now he saw a jackal trotting along the forest path and he called out, 'Uncle Jackal, you of all creatures of the wild have not given judgment between the lion and myself.' Once again he told his story. 'Is it justice that, in return for my kindness, he should eat me?' Jabulani concluded.

The jackal thought for several minutes before giving his reply. When he did so he shook his head, put on a perplexed expression, and said, 'It is difficult for me, Jabulani, to speak on such a matter, for I do not understand how the lion came to be in the trap. Let us go to the trap, so that I may see what you mean.'

So the lion and Jabulani led the jackal back to the trap.

'Now,' said the jackal to the lion, 'where exactly were you when you called to Jabulani to release you? Were you actually inside the trap?'

'Yes,' answered the lion, 'I was inside the trap.'

'But I cannot understand how, let alone why, you got to be there. Show me how you got in.'

The lion explained that the hunter had set bait to lure animals into the trap. And he jumped into the trap to show the jackal how it worked. However, Jackal was still not satisfied. 'But was the trapdoor open, or was it closed?'

'It was closed,' said the lion, sounding rather annoyed with this lengthy process.

'Well close it, Jabulani, so that I might see exactly what the lion means,' went on the jackal. The boy needed no second invitation and, as the heavy door fell back into place, Jackal laughed heartily, 'Goodbye, oh foolish one! You may stay there till you die, for it is not right that you should return evil for good, no matter how hungry you may be!'

Jabulani thanked the clever little jackal for saving his life, and for bringing justice to the treacherous lion.

How fire was discovered

A TSWANA TALE

The BaTswana will tell you that when the first man lived on the earth, he was unaware of the power of fire or how to make it. He was, in fact, unaware of its existence. In the beginning all he ate were the roots, bulbs and fruits provided by Mother Nature in the bush that surrounded him. If he ate any meat he did so raw, but most of the time he relied on one of the greatest gifts provided by Modimo, the 'Hidden One', as they called the Creator, which was cow's milk.

Milk was the daily drink of both young and old.

There was little to trouble Man, for the sun kept him warm by day and animal skins kept him warm by night. In the beginning the weather did not vary much between summer and winter and the climate was not as extreme as it can be today. Life was good, and Man felt most fortunate indeed.

But it came to pass that one day dawned much colder than was usual, and the clouds were thick in the sky. Man gathered up his spear and decided to go off in search of food. He travelled far, much further than he usually went. All the landmarks were new to him, and there was an eerie silence. He paused to listen. The stillness was unfamiliar, so he scanned the countryside ahead of him until he saw a tall, thin cloud slowly spiralling up into the heavens.

'This is most strange,' he thought to himself. 'Never before have I seen such a sight. Clouds do not go straight upwards; this one seems to come out of the very Earth itself! I must go and find out about this.'

He approached the place of the cloud slowly, in awe and reverence, and the nearer he got the more intriguing the sight became until he found, on the threshold of a cave, a fire burning cheerfully. All the while there rose from the fire a thin wisp of smoke. It rose up to the sky.

Good manners were natural to Man, so he greeted the fire civilly. 'Good day to you stranger!' he said. 'I have lived in this land since the day of Creation, since all drew their first breath, but I have never seen or heard of your kind before. Pray tell me, to whom do I speak?'

'I return your courteous greeting, Two-Legged-One,' replied Fire pleasantly. 'I am one of Modimo's many servants. Come nearer, for the day is cold. You are welcome to warm yourself in my smile.'

The man got closer to the fire, and his cold body was at once comforted by the heat of the fire that warmed him on the side closest to the flame. He sat down on his haunches for a while to enjoy the good company of the stranger and the two chattered away for some time. As the man became warmer, his feeling of contentment grew. He thought how pleasant it would be if his new friend would visit his home so that his wife and children could experience the same pleasure that radiated out from this unusual friend. He was beginning to hope, secretly, that he could keep this friend forever.

So, before he left, the man extended an invitation to Fire to come and visit him at his home. He promised Fire a kindly welcome, not only from himself, but from his wife and children too. But, to his great disappointment, the fire declined his invitation. However, Fire assured the man of a cordial reception at any time should he wish to return on future visits.

Man returned home full of wonder at what he had seen, and could not wait to tell his family and friends about his adventure.

'He was beautiful beyond description,' the man told his wife. 'He wore a red and yellow wrap; his laughter crackled; many little stars drifted upwards from the ever-changing shape of his mouth. But you should have seen his breath! It gathered like a cloud that never stopped rising to the heavens, but when the breeze blew some over me, I could not stop coughing! How he laughed at that!'

'Husband, I am filled with great curiosity to see this wonderful creature. Can you not bring him to visit us?'

The man told his wife that Fire had refused his invitation, but he promised he would try again. This he did, not just once, but on the many occasions when he returned to further his friendship with this wonderful creature. But each time he requested the pleasure of Fire's company, the fire found some reason to excuse himself.

And each time Man returned from his visits he had new wonders to tell of. Eventually his wife and children begged so desperately to see this wondrous friend that the next time he visited Fire, he had tears in his eyes. Worried, the fire asked what the matter was.

'Why,' Man pleaded, 'do you continue to refuse my offers of hospitality? Am I not your friend?'

'Yes, you are indeed my friend,' the fire assured him, 'and it hurts me to refuse your wish. You must bear with me and be patient if I seem ungracious.

The truth is that I am frightened to leave my home for, whenever I do, a trail of destruction follows me.'

'That would be nothing compared to the joy that your presence would give to my wife and children,' the man assured him. So, after a great deal of persuasion and hesitation, a day was finally set. The man was overjoyed and ran all the way back home to give his family the great news.

When the momentous day arrived the whole village was in an uproar of excitement and a sumptuous feast was prepared in honour of their guest. Everything was made ready many hours beforehand.

Fire left his cave in a quiet, orderly manner, but as he made his way along the pathway that had become worn between his home and that of his human friend, his fingers brushed against the tinder-dry grass that grew all along the path. They fed it into his ever-hungry mouth. As he went, he grew in stature, and as he grew, so did his hunger.

From the grass along the path, the snatching fingers grasped the nearby bushes, and these were also fed to the voracious mouth. Soon the bushes proved too small, so Fire fed on trees. As he progressed, so he grew ever larger. And as he grew, a wind sprang up behind him to speed him on his way. Soon the whole countryside was ablaze.

In the distance Man and his family, waiting in their hut, glimpsed the quiet departure of Fire from his home, his presence a small plume of smoke rising into the sky.

'My friend comes!' called out the man excitedly. 'See, that is his breath, just as I told you. Soon you will see how truly beautiful he is. Look how he dances on his way. He is happy to be visiting us!'

'Yes, he is beautiful indeed,' exclaimed his wife and children, though the sight made them feel somewhat uncertain. 'We are most honoured that he should visit us.'

But as the clouds of smoke began to billow up into the heavens in dense plumes the scene became more ominous. Birds flew past in terror, trying to escape the pursuing flames. Antelope with heaving sides fled to escape the scorching blaze. All tried to run from this monster that they did not understand. Even Man's precious cows began to low in distress, and soon fled for their lives with their calves. Man and his family listened in fear to the mighty roar of the fire as it bore down upon them.

'Husband!' cried the now terrified wife, 'are you sure that your friend means us no harm? See how your children cower in fear.'

'I too am afraid,' said the man, ' for I have never seen Fire in such a mood!'

The man ran out towards Fire, shouting, pleading with him to return home and do them no harm, but, if he had to continue forth, then to become calmer.

Fire was deaf to his pleas and, if anything, grew in intensity, until at last all in his path was consumed.

The man and his family now took to their heels and followed the birds and animals in fleeing before the flames. But as they ran, the fire gained upon them. Then, as their skin was beginning to scorch, they reached a broad, shallow river crossing. They splashed through the water and it soothed their heated skins.

The cool, clear river water revived them and, as they hurried on, the man looked behind them and was surprised to see that the fire was no longer following them.

'What miracle is this?' cried the man, as he tried to calm the sobbing child that he carried. 'The water has saved us. The one who I thought was my friend has not followed us across the river. He is afraid. And look, our precious cattle are safe on this side of the river! We are saved!' And they threw themselves on the dry ground and hugged each other, weeping tears of joy.

The fire slowly died out as it reached the edge of the river, although tree trunks blazed far into the night, flickering out only as a new day dawned.

Man went back to his home that day, which was an ugly, charred and blackened wasteland as far as the eye could see. Inside the skeleton of the poles that had been his hut were the remnants of his family's belongings and those of the feast that had been prepared for their honoured guest.

The man picked up the charred remains of one of the roots. It gave forth a delicious aroma, so he put it in his mouth and bit it.

'Wife!' he exclaimed with surprise, 'The feast that awaited our guest has not spoiled; indeed, it has been improved! Come, let us eat it, for there is nothing else left in this desolation that can satisfy our hunger. But,' he added, 'never, never again will I ask that demon of destruction to visit our home!'

And so it was that man learned to improve his food by cooking it, and how to quench fire with water. First he roasted the roots and vegetables that grew in the bush, and then he learnt to cook the raw flesh of the animals that he kept and hunted. Today, fire is one of Modimo's most valued gifts to man.

The Tswana

The ancestors of the Tswana migrated from the north about 600 years ago, moving south into the modern country of Botswana and beyond. They were part of a mass migration that moved through the centre of the continent. The BaTswana are very conservative. The heads of each BaTswana clan meet in a gathering of the tribal elders known as a *kgotla*. At these meetings the daily life of the clan is discussed and a consensus of opinion sought before decisions are made. This is a time-consuming but highly democratic process.

The BaTswana are traditionally farmers, and cattle husbandry has dominated their culture for centuries. The men used to hunt while the women tilled the fields, grew the crops and took care of all the domestic activities. The tradition of ancestor worship is strong among the BaTswana; belief in witchcraft and in the power of sorcerers is a persistent element in their daily life.

How Snake lost his legs

A BUSHMAN TALE

Long ago there was a terrible drought. The Moon looked down on the earth with pity and told Mantis, 'You must go with your wives and children and all the animals and all the beasts and move from this land. Soon there will be nothing here but desert.'

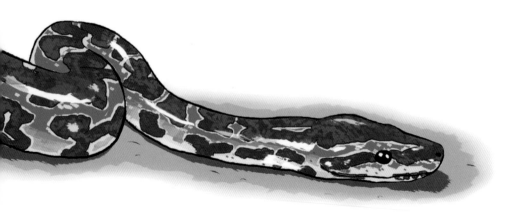

Mantis did as he was told, and soon all the animals had gathered together all their belongings and trekked away to safer places. All, that is, but Snake. In those ancient days, Snake had four legs like all the other animals. But Snake, as everyone knew, was lazy and chose not to believe Mantis.

'No, I will stay here. Your drought will not worry me,' he said.

But soon the last of the grass shrivelled up and died and still the rain did not fall. The fat little frogs had hopped away and the snake started to get thinner and thinner. He had never known such terrible hunger.

Finally, he decided to follow in the footsteps of the other, wiser animals that had listened to Mantis's warning. But by now the land was a desert, and with each tired step the snake sank into the hot sand. Every step was a wearisome task. At last in desperation Snake cried out, 'Oh Moon! I am ashamed of myself. Save me from the sun and I will change my ways!'

The Moon took pity on the creature, and in a flash the snake found that his legs had shrunk away to nothing. On his gleaming belly, he could glide across the hot sand with ease without sinking in as he had done before. So off went the snake. Slithering silently across the hot sands, he found his way out of the desert, and so, like the other animals, he was saved.

We don't know if Snake really did change his ways. But, to this day, the San still do not look kindly upon these creatures, so it is just possible that he continues to be as lazy as ever.

The insect that eats its partner

Large Green Praying Mantis

Sphodromantis gastrica

Praying mantises are carnivorous (meat-eating) insects that stalk their prey, often standing with a slight swaying motion, their forelegs folded in front, their head tilted on a flexible neck. Their 'praying' posture and large compound eyes give an impression of great wisdom. The name of their order in the insect world, Mantodea, comes from the Greek for 'prophet' or 'soothsayer'.

When prey comes within the mantis's reach, it shoots out surprisingly long arms to seize the victim with a double row of spikes and swiftly pull it to its mouth. Although the mandibles of the jaw are small, they nibble fast, and soon the prey is munched into a pulp and swallowed. Usually only tough legs and wings remain uneaten.

Mantises seem fearless and can catch and eat prey as large as themselves. If threatened, they strike out with their forelimbs and can even draw blood. Some species flash their wings open to reveal brightly coloured patterns resembling threatening eyes, which are especially effective at warning off birds.

The male is smaller than the female, who normally kills and eats her mate – sometimes even while mating is in progress! Newly hatched mantises are usually black and have no wings. They quickly disperse and set off on their own – before their mother can eat them.

The Large Green Mantis is a common species and usually hides in the foliage of trees and shrubs. It eats caterpillars as well as adult insects, which plague farmers, and is therefore a beneficial insect.

The Bushmen

The Bushmen, or San as they are also known, were the first of the modern human inhabitants of southern and East Africa.

The San were hunter-gatherers, living in small, nomadic bands – extended families – that roamed the great sunlit spaces in freedom and in total harmony with the land, its plants and animals.

Generally, the men were concerned with the hunt; the women would wander near the encampment in search of plants and roots. However, there were no strict divisions based on gender: the San had a profound belief in sharing, in co-operation within the family, between clan and clan, as well as between humans and the environment. Water was of supreme importance. The rains in southern Africa are highly seasonal and often unreliable, and the clans were skilled in locating and preserving the precious sources of moisture, which often lay beneath the dry surface. And they followed the rains.

Theirs was a highly mobile way of life. Their homes were temporary and simple: grass shelters that were occupied for no more than a couple of months at the most. Possessions were only those essential to survival, for, whatever you owned, you had to carry. Belongings were limited to the tools needed for hunting and digging, and animal skins for clothing, blankets, carrying bags and pouches. Adornments were also sparse, comprising perhaps an ostrich or snail shell.

The San often used caves rather than man-made shelters. In these we find the works of art that served as the link between the living and the spirit worlds. Painted or, sometimes, scratched out of the rock, they often depict the mythical creatures and heroes that populate the San fables.

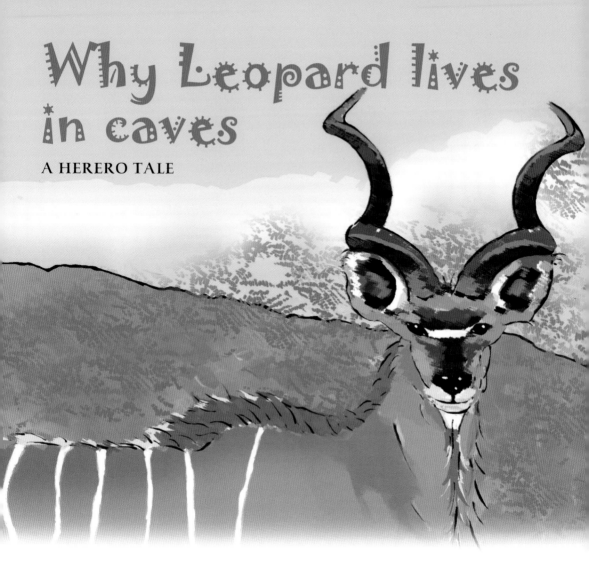

Why Leopard lives in caves

A HERERO TALE

Long ago, at the beginning of time, the kudu found a perfect place to build a hut. It was on a grassy knoll, it was protected from the elements, and it was sheltered and secure. It even had a stream of cool, clear running water nearby.

Kudu was delighted with his new place. He decided it was perfect, and that his long, hard search for an ideal site for his home had been rewarded. Determined to lose no more time, he took an axe and set off into the surrounding forest to cut poles to build his hut. If you want to build a house, the first thing you do is cut nice straight poles for a stout frame.

Not long after he had left, Leopard approached the grassy knoll from the opposite direction. After he had lain down for a while, he also thought this was the ideal place to build a home. Though Leopard was a lazy animal, he wanted this spot for himself, so he decided that the hard work of building a house would be well worth the effort. He, too, took an axe and he set off back into the forest to cut some poles to begin building a frame.

Kudu cut a nice straight sapling. He lopped off its branches, and when it was smooth and straight, he carried it back up to the grassy knoll. He then returned to cut another.

On the other side of the hill, the leopard had also prepared a straight pole, trimmed nice and smooth, and he carried it back to the chosen spot. As he laid it down in the shade of the tree, he was most surprised to see a pole already there, smooth and trimmed; a perfect pole to build a hut with!

'Well! What a stroke of luck! That will help me build my home,' thought the leopard. He then returned to his side of the hill to cut more poles.

Meanwhile Kudu had prepared his second pole, which he carried back to place with the first one. Only when he put it down did he realize that there were three poles, and not just two! This had him perplexed for a while, but he accepted what he saw and was soon off to cut a fourth. Clearly his memory was failing him and, anyway, he did not have time to ponder the mystery – he was too busy home-building.

Leopard returned to the hill feeling rather hot and sweaty. Home-building was hard work, something he was not used to. 'Well, that is three poles cut now,' he thought to himself. But what was this? Leopard still had his second pole over his shoulder, yet there were now three poles lying on the ground. Leopard put the fourth pole down and contemplated the mystery. The first explanation that jumped into his mind was that the place must be bewitched – and that was an alarming thought! But as he pondered further on the subject the answer came to him. It was obvious! Naturally, the Ancestors would wish to help him build his home. This had to be their doing. And this made Leopard extremely happy, especially when he considered all the hard work it would save him. So he left the pole with the others and off he went.

'One, two, three, four … FIVE! How can such a thing be?' worried Kudu when he returned to the hill? Bewitchment was also his first conclusion, but who had ever heard of such a thing actually helping anybody! 'By the Spirits of my Ancestors,' he exclaimed, 'who can be responsible for this?' Then Kudu realized he had answered his own question. Why, it had to be his Ancestors show-ing approval for his choice of home. Greatly pleased, Kudu returned to his task with renewed vigour.

By dusk, there were enough poles for the frame of a hut. Both animals were exhausted and each found a comfortable patch of long grass to sleep in, each dreaming contentedly of a splendid group of Ancestors toiling away to help make this fine new home.

The next morning, Kudu was up at first light to cut a bundle of grass with which to thatch the roof. He brought the bundle back before setting out again. No sooner had he left, than Leopard arrived and, pleased to see the Ancestors' gift of some thatching grass, started to knock the main posts of the hut into the ground. This was hot, thirsty work, so he went down to the stream for a drink.

When Kudu returned with another huge bundle of thatching grass he was amazed to see that the Ancestors had started to build the frame of his hut. Kudu hurriedly finished placing the remaining poles in the ground and then went to collect more thatch. Leopard then returned and began to weave the thinner poles into the uprights to make the walls ready to be daubed with mud. This was really tiring work and soon Leopard departed for a rest by the river, secretly hoping that the Ancestors would complete the task. And wouldn't you know it? They did just that!

Leopard soon learnt that if he came early in the cool of the morning and did a little work on the frame, or brought some reeds or thatching grass, then he could find a shady spot and rest for the remainder of the day. The Ancestors would just carry on with the work. Now *this* was the way to build a home!

And each morning Kudu was overjoyed to see that his Ancestors had not neglected him, but had provided something for the house, and he would toil hard for the rest of the day, happy in this knowledge.

By the end of the week the last bundle of thatch had been tied in place and the hut was now completed and ready to be occupied. Kudu looked at it with pride and said, 'Oh, my great and noble Ancestors, this is indeed a fine house and I am most grateful for your help.' He walked around the hut three times, then entered and fell fast asleep.

Not long afterwards, just as it was getting dark, Leopard came to see the hut. It was still light enough to see that it was a very fine hut indeed. He also walked around the hut three times, and then he, too, entered. It was pitch dark inside, but Leopard decided that his hut was completed. He lay down and was soon fast asleep, dreaming of his illustrious Ancestors and all their help. He dreamt of handsome, many-spotted leopards dancing around the hut, but one came forwards towards him, and as it got nearer it lost its spots and turned into a kudu. Leopard could not suppress a shrill scream.

Kudu had also been dreaming of his Ancestors: they were sitting outside, in a circle around the hut, waiting for someone to come out. But who could that person be? The suspense was intolerable and he could not contain himself. 'Whoever you are,' he shouted, 'make yourself known!' But all he heard was a faint scream.

Kudu, now wide awake, lay in the dark. He thought he could make out the shape of a crouched figure near the doorway. He knew the scream had been real, but he pinched himself to make sure he was not still dreaming. 'Ow!' he squealed loudly, for the pinch had hurt!

'Oh dear!' said Leopard, who was also wide awake now and very alarmed. 'Who is that?'

'What are you doing in my house?' demanded the kudu.

'I am Ngwi, the leopard, and this is my house!'

'It is not! It is my house,' snapped Kudu.

'How dare you? I cut poles, I cut grass, I …'

'Rubbish!' interrupted the kudu, 'I cut poles, and cut the grass and built the house. I, and my Ancestors.'

'You and your Ancestors, my spots!' exclaimed the leopard indignantly. 'Who knocked the first poles into the ground?'

'Well, who did then?'

'I did!' proclaimed the leopard triumphantly. 'It is my home!'

'*You* knocked the first poles into the ground? You and not my Ancestors?' the kudu was beginning to see what had happened. 'Well, then who put up the other poles and did all the thatching?'

'I did, of course!' said the leopard.

'You? Are you sure of that?' pressed the kudu.

'Well, not exactly. My own Ancestors did a bit of the work, but that is the same thing!' continued the leopard defensively.

'Would it be of interest for you to know that it was I, Kudu, who cut the first pole, who did almost all the work, did all the thatching? It was I who …'

'But it could not have been. You are not one of my Ancestors!' Leopard retorted.

'I should hope not!' snorted the kudu, perhaps unwisely. 'But get this into your head: it was I who found the place first and did most of the work, so it will be I who lives here!'

'Well, I am going to live in it,' snarled the leopard, offended by Kudu's reference to the leopard Ancestors.

'Who is going to live in what?' chimed in Hare, who had just arrived on the scene. He had been looking for his friend, the kudu, for days and had at last tracked him down. 'My! My!' said Hare, noticing the structure. 'What a fine house.'

'Yes, I built it,' said Kudu quickly, 'The trouble is that Ngwi claims it because he cut a few poles and knocked the first few into the ground. But I got here first, cut the first pole and did most of the work! So it is mine, is it not?'

'It sounds like you both had better tell me the whole story,' said the hare. And so they did, detail by detail.

Hare listened carefully to Kudu and Leopard as they described events in the order they happened. Then Hare made his pronouncement. 'To me, it sounds as though you both had a hand in making the house, so you each have a share in it. Live in it together!'

'What? Me live with the leopard?' exclaimed the kudu, who was not at ease with such a solution.

'What? Me live with a kudu?' cried the leopard, equally unhappy.

'Yes, and I am sure you will find a way to live with each other comfortably!' said the hare. 'And now I must be on my way. Perhaps, Ngwi, you will walk with me a short way, as there is a matter I wish to discuss with you. Goodbye Kudu, I hope to come and visit you in *your* home soon.'

Kudu looked at the hare. The way he had said 'your' home made him wonder if Hare was up to one of his deceptions, but on whom? Hare just gazed at Kudu, grinned and then winked as he walked away with the leopard. At first they chatted about the weather and other casual things and then Hare made some complimentary remarks about the new hut.

'You will find Kudu a fine fellow to live with,' Hare added. 'I am sure that you will get on very well. But there is one thing that you must watch for. Kudu does fly into terrible fits of rage. Not often, mind you! But sometimes the strangest little things set him off. When his temper gets the better of him he lowers his head and charges, horns first! He really can be dangerous when he is like this. You must be most careful. He could kill you!'

'Oh! How dreadful! I had no idea Kudu could be like this!' Now Leopard was really concerned.

'I thought as much, so I wanted you to be warned. Do not let it worry you, just be careful, that is all. The signs are usually quite clear when he is about to charge as he usually backs off a little before coming at you. My advice is, if you see his horns go down and point at you and he backs away, then run for your life!'

With that, Hare wished Leopard well and left him. Leopard went back to the hut and from then on he watched the kudu continuously, never taking his eyes off the antelope. Those huge curved horns were most worrying. On one occasion, when they were walking along a track in the forest, Kudu stepped backwards to avoid some thorns in the path – and Leopard nearly fainted. He jumped back several feet.

'Whatever is the matter?' said the kudu. 'Did something alarm you?'

'No, no!' replied the leopard a bit too quickly, 'I like to jump! See!' And Leopard started jumping up and down on the spot. This happened several times that day, and it started to puzzle the kudu. 'Do you have to do that?' he complained. 'It annoys me!'

'Oh dear!' worried the leopard. This arrangement to share the house was not going at all well.

Then a storm gathered. There were huge claps of thunder, and then a torrential downpour. Leopard and Kudu rushed to the house for cover. They became worried that the tempest would destroy their new home, but it stood up well and passed the test. In fact, the rain had helped to settle the thatch. When the storm had passed, they went outside to see if any other damage had occurred. All was well apart from the track to the house, which had become a gushing stream, and had loosened the stones and boulders. Kudu slipped and slithered as he went down the gully.

'Be careful not to loosen any rocks as you go along!' warned the kudu, but too late. The leopard stood on a large rock that wobbled, and then slid down the path, straight at Kudu, and knocked him over.

'OW!' Kudu yelped. 'HELP!' And he stood up and checked himself for any major injuries. He shook his legs, but no serious damage had been done. 'That could have broken my leg, you clumsy cat!' he complained bitterly.

'Oh my!' Leopard thought to himself, 'now I have really made him angry!'

Kudu began to regain his footing but the soft mud made him slip and slide. He could not make his way up, not slowly. 'I will never get back unless I really rush at the slope,' he thought.

All that Leopard could see was the kudu lower his head, point his horns in Leopard's direction, and start backing up. Now Leopard was terrified! This was exactly what Hare had warned him about and he vividly recalled what the hare had told him: 'Get out of his way!'

With a loud snort, Kudu came bounding up the slope and, with a yelp of fear, the leopard bounded off down the slope in the opposite direction. Leopard ran, and ran, and ran. He ran until he was exhausted and could run no more! He found a quiet, dry cave and hid inside, thinking to himself, 'There is no way that I am going back, not if Kudu can turn nasty like that for no real reason. No house is worth that kind of torment!'

By the time Kudu reached the top of the slope he, too, was tired from his exertions, and Leopard was nowhere to be seen. Kudu did not think much of

the leopard's absence, and he went into the hut to clean himself up and rest.

Several days later, Hare dropped by to visit his friend, the kudu, and asked how life was treating him in his new home.

Kudu told Hare that the house was wonderful. It had proved very sturdy, he said, even under the test of a severe storm. But he was perplexed that Leopard was nowhere to be found.

'I hear he is now living in a cave, far from here!' chuckled the hare.

'Oh! Then does that mean the house is mine alone?' queried the kudu with great interest.

'I suppose so,' said the hare. 'Rumour has it that he will never come back.'

'Not ever? Really, not at all?' wondered Kudu, unable to believe his good fortune. 'I cannot help but be glad, for I did not like sharing with him. He was such a bag of nerves! Maybe it was all the thunder and lightning that scared him away!'

'Maybe it was you!' suggested Hare as he departed with a grin and a wink.

And ever since that day Leopard has preferred to live on his own, in the safety of a cave, with only himself for company!

The Grey Ghost of Africa

Greater kudu

Tragelaphus strepsiceros

The kudu is one of the larger members of the antelope family, its range extending from South Africa's Eastern Cape Province as far north as Ethiopia. It thrives in the savanna, is especially well adapted to rugged, hilly areas, and is quite happy living close to human activity.

Males and females differ considerably, in both looks and behaviour. The males are much larger, have magnificent spiral horns, a prominent mane of hair down the back and throat, and are greyish-brown (hence their 'Grey Ghost' nickname). Females are cinnamon coloured. They live with their offspring in orderly family groups, in a well-defined home range; males, however, wander over much larger tracts of land. They form loose coalitions with other males, usually of a similar age, and mix with the female herd only in the breeding season. At these times there are sometimes fierce fights between males. In fact, there have been cases of males that have locked horns and, unable to separate, have died as a consequence.

The kudu is renowned for its ability to jump even high game-fences and can easily clear obstacles two metres high. Both sexes have large, rounded ears and excellent senses of hearing and smell. The white stripes on their coats break up their outlines in thick bush and so help with camouflage.

When Bat was a Bird

A NDEBELE TALE

The ancient ones tell us that, in the beginning, Lulwane the bat had his place with the bird people. All used to admire him for his beauty and especially for the colour of his plumage, which was varied and shone like burnished metal in the African sunlight. But for those that admired him – and there were many – few could be said to have liked Lulwane, for his greed and selfishness were common knowledge.

Lulwane would never share his feeding grounds with others when food was scarce in the land. He would deliberately leave his roost in the trees long before first light, while the other creatures of the bush were still asleep, so that they would never see the direction in which he went.

Then came the Great Drought.

The months passed and no rain fell to cool the parched earth or swell the hard seeds and fruit of the bush. The pools and pans received no water and, as the merciless sun shone down with no respite, they began to dry up.

Starvation threatened to spread throughout the land, but Lulwane remained sleek and fat, while the others became thin and haggard. Eventually, the other animals drove Lulwane away because of his greed and selfishness.

Lulwane found a cave, and used it as both his home and his hideaway. If anything, he became even more secretive in his movements. Earlier and earlier each night he would begin his forays in search of food, flying swiftly to his destination, and stopping nowhere else, for he no longer wished to meet with his former friends. Longer and longer he would fly around during the hours of darkness, and his eyesight became as keen as that of the owl, who sees by night. During the day, Lulwane would hide away in the darkest recesses of his cave so that the sun could not hurt his sensitive eyes. He would sleep away the daylight hours.

Yet even though he had all the food he could eat, he could find no water, and what use is food without water to drink? A little dew fell at night-time, but dew was difficult to collect before it fell from the leaves to soak into the parched soil. All the beasts and birds were in a sorry state, even the well-fed Lulwane.

But among the animal people there was a tribe that was smarter than the others. This was the tribe of the Gundwane, the rats. The rats also had nimble hands. They were not afraid to work hard, and were known to be driven by their thirst. And so it was that the rat people had banded together to make a smooth, rounded basin in the dry river bed. They pounded the shape of a basin with their small hands, and they lined it with clay from some of the bigger water holes, those that had not dried to the hardness of rock. Now they were able to catch the life-giving dew that fell each night; rather than seeping away, the liquid now slipped down the sides of the clay-lined basin and gathered in a pool. Each dawn saw a crystal-clear liquid in sufficient quantity that all could slake their thirst. And all the animals of the bush showered the Gundwane with praises for their clever invention.

Now Lulwane would come to the dew pool each night to slake his thirst, and he would drink in the dark and share the water with the Gundwane, who were also creatures of the night. As time passed, he became more like the rat people, both in appearance and sound, and mingled with them unnoticed at the water's edge.

'Now,' said Lulwane, 'I will leave my people for good and become like the rat. Who among the bird people could have provided water to quench the thirst of all the many animals of the bush? For sure the Gundwane have the brains to surpass all others!'

But, in some ways, old habits die hard. With the coming of each new day, the Gundwane returned to their holes in the ground and slept away the hours of daylight. This Lulwane could not do, for he knew nothing about holes in the ground, and he continued to retire to his cave when the first light of day reached the horizon. As the rocky recesses had no boughs to perch on, he learnt to cling to the roof of the cave and sleep suspended upside down, and he sleeps in this way to this very day.

As time passed, Lulwane the bat lost the colours of his splendid plumage. No longer did his feathers shine in the sunlight and, starved of sunlight, they withered and failed to grow. Instead, to protect himself from the cold of the dark caves, he grew a cover of warm, grey fur. His wings were reduced to webbed skin, and his beak disappeared to form the snout of today's bat.

But still Lulwane flies with speed and great agility, just as Sedhlu, the honeyguide, does. So who can possibly deny that Lulwane the bat was once one of the bird people?

The most quarrelsome of animals

Peters' Epauletted Fruit Bat

Epomophorus crypturus

Southern Africa is home to eight members of the fruit bat family, of which Peters' Epauletted is the commonest. These little mammals roost in trees in large colonies, several hundred strong, hanging upside down by their feet with their 'wings' wrapped around themselves. The colonies are very noisy. In fact there's nothing noisier in the animal world than a garrulous fruit bat trying to grab the best roosting position, and then trying to keep it.

As their name suggests, they are predominantly fruit eaters, though they also eat flowers, buds and nectar. They are wasteful feeders and the ground beneath a feeding post is often strewn with bits of skin, seeds and chewed-up pulp, as if they are just squeezing out the juices and discarding the flesh of the fruit. Figs are their favourite meal.

Fruit bats have two claws on each wing, pointed dog-like snouts, and coats that can vary in colour but are mostly a brownish buff. The larger males have scent glands on their shoulders, which are covered in long white hairs. When the bat gets excited or is threatened, these glands turn inside out and this makes the conspicuous white 'epaulette'.

The Motherly Baboon

A ZULU TALE

Kulumele gave birth to a handsome baby son whom she named Mpabane. When he was two months old she could no longer be excused from the seasonal task of hoeing the millet lands, so she put the baby across her back and secured him to her with a braided goatskin *kaross*

in the traditional manner. Kulumele knew that the gentle rhythm of her body as she hoed would quickly lull the little boy to sleep.

But Kulumele had not counted on the sun being so hot. It beat down upon them mercilessly, and before long Mpabane was screaming with discomfort.

Kulumele was unsure what to do as the rains were not far off and she was late in getting her lands ready for sowing. She saw a large tree nearby that had deep shade beneath its spreading canopy, so she placed the goatskin *kaross* in the coolness, laid her baby on it and returned to her labours. She sang loudly as she worked so that her son could hear her voice and sleep contentedly.

Not far away lived a troop of fierce baboons ruled by a cruel leader called Nymphere. But one of them was different from the others, and she was called Fenisana. She was kind and gentle, loving all the living creatures of the wild. While the rest of the troop hurt the smaller creatures in cruel play, Fenisana would snatch them away and hold them close to her, later setting them free in the safety of the forest.

All the newborn baboon babies were entrusted to her care. Fenisana loved their helplessness and would sit for hours rocking them back and forth in her arms, crooning to them in a gruff but kind voice whilst their mothers romped and played in the senseless and foolish way of monkeys.

One day, Fenisana wandered farther away than usual from the troop and paused in the coolness of the huge shady tree. She was overcome with joy to see the sleeping form of Mpabane. Gently she picked up the baby and rocked him in her lap, making her funny grunting noises to him.

After a while, Kulumele paused to rest her aching back and glanced towards the shady tree – and saw the baboon. With a shriek of fear she dropped her hoe and rushed towards the tree to snatch her baby from the fearsome creature's grasp.

'Aye!' she screamed, 'leave my baby alone! Who are you?'

To her immense surprise the baboon replied, 'I am Fenisana. Please let me nurse your child. I love the little one!'

But Kulumele snatched her little boy away, and hurried back to her kraal.

The following day she found Fenisana waiting for her under the spreading tree, and as they approached, the baboon stretched out her arms and said, 'Please let me hold your baby while you work. No harm will come to him. Let me guard him for you!'

'How strange,' thought Kulumele aloud. 'She speaks as if she is a human. Surely she would make a perfect nurse for my child.' So she placed her son in the outstretched arms, and all through the long morning Fenisana cared tenderly for the baby.

When the midday hour came, Kulumele took Fenisana by the hand and led her to the kraal. There she gave the baboon her porridge scrapings and a bowl of curdled milk, and afterwards the baboon settled down happily to nurse the child once more.

Soon it was time for the evening meal and Kulumele busied herself with the cooking pot, but when she left the hut to call her husband to eat and to fetch her baby, there was no sign of either the baboon or her son. Fearing her husband's anger at entrusting the safety of their only child to a wild creature, she quickly found a long, smooth rock, which she wrapped in the goatskin *kaross* and slung like a baby across her back. Then, pretending that all was as it should be, she called the man to come and eat.

Later, when all had settled down to sleep, Kulumele crooned to the rock from time to time, just as she would have done to her baby. Then she quietly slipped out of the hut and walked to the forest where she knew the fierce Nymphere, the baboon leader, lived.

Through the dark, eerie forest she stumbled, calling at every step, 'Fenisana, Fenisana, where are you? Where is my son?'

Eventually, from the distance, she heard Fenisana reply, 'Here I am. Here I am, and so too is your child!'

With a cry of relief and joy, Kulumele stumbled on through the darkness in the direction of the voice and soon found herself in a clearing in the bush. The baboon troop was sitting in a circle, and in the centre was Fenisana, cradling her

little one. But when Kulumele tried to take away her son, the baboons closed in around her, and their chief, the feared Nymphere, caught her roughly by the arm.

'Your son belongs to us now,' he shouted, 'to guide us in your human ways when I am old. The brains of a man and the strength of a baboon, that will make us lords over all the other beasts!'

The big baboon continued, 'I have a need too! For human flesh. This I have not tasted since I was young. Your meat should be both soft and sweet. Tomorrow *you* will provide us with a feast!' And then Nymphere added, looking around the circle with his wicked eyes, 'Should anyone here allow the captives to escape, theirs will be the meat that provides the feast!'

With these ominous words, all the baboons shuddered in fear. Nymphere then commanded his subjects to hold Kulumele, whilst he bound and tied her tightly with long, strong creepers from the nearby trees.

Throughout all this, poor Fenisana wept bitterly. She had not thought her naughtiness in taking the baby would turn so sour. When all was quiet and the rest of the troop slept, she crept up to Kulumele's side and, one by one, she gnawed through the bindings with her sharp young teeth. As soon as Kulumele was free, Fenisana clasped Mpabane tightly to her and then carefully led Kulumele through the sleeping, prostrate forms and out of the dark forest to the kraal. Gently, she placed the baby into his mother's arms, and silently disappeared back into the darkness.

When Kulumele's husband heard of all that had happened, he killed his fattest cow in gratitude to Fenisana and all the village came to a great feast, one that lasted for many days.

As for Fenisana, she had made amends for the irresponsible act that had so nearly ended up in disaster. But we shall never know if she escaped the wrath of the evil Nymphere. Only the animals of the wild can tell us that.

Lessons from primates

Chacma Baboon

Papio ursinus

The Chacma is the only member of the baboon family, and the largest primate, other than humans, in southern Africa. They are intelligent animals, able to exploit man's activities. For example, dams and farming development have enabled them to expand their range. Given water and trees or cliffs to bed down in, they can flourish nearly anywhere, except for extreme deserts or high forests.

Baboons live in large groups (averaging 38 individuals) and have evolved a complex social behaviour, giving insight into the way our own distant ancestors behaved. Living in large groups provides safety in numbers and vigilance against threat; but it also means competition for food. Baboons form allegiances by grooming one another, and by investing time and effort in cultivating allies.

Within a troop, males are dominant to females, but females cultivate special relationships with senior males in order to enhance their position.

Researchers believe that our early hominid ancestors also needed to form strong bonds and alliances as they moved from the forest and into the open savanna.

The Tortoise and the Baboon

A SHONA TALE

On a pleasant evening many a long day ago, Tortoise was making his way home in his usual slow crawl when he met Baboon on the path.

'Hello old friend! Have you found much to eat today?' the baboon enquired heartily.

'No,' replied the tortoise, 'very little indeed!'

The baboon started to dance up and down, chortling with laughter at an idea that had just come into his head.

'Follow me, poor old Tortoise,' he said, 'and when you reach my home I will have all the supper you can eat ready for you!'

'Thank you! Thank you!' replied a most grateful tortoise, and the baboon spun around gleefully and then started quickly down the path that led home.

Tortoise followed as quickly as he could, which was very slowly indeed, especially when he had to climb a hill. Once or twice, when the ground became bumpier, he had to stop for a rest and became disheartened, but, keeping the picture of a wonderful feast in his mind, he continued to plod bravely on.

At last Tortoise reached the place in the bush that Baboon called home. And there was Baboon, leaping and cavorting around with a grin fixed on his face.

'Well, bless my bent tail! What a long time you've taken to get here. It must be tomorrow already!'

'I am so sorry!' puffed Tortoise, who was still recovering from his long journey. 'But I'm sure you have had plenty of time to prepare the supper. Please do not grumble at me!'

'Oh yes indeed!' replied the baboon, rubbing his hands together. 'The supper is prepared. All you have to do is climb up and get it – see!' and he pointed up into the topmost branches of the huge old tree. 'Three pots of millet beer,' he continued, 'brewed especially for you.'

The poor old tortoise looked longingly up into the tall tree where Baboon had wedged the three pots in the branches far above their heads. He knew he could never reach them, and Baboon knew that too.

'Be a good friend and bring one down for me,' begged Tortoise. But the baboon clambered up the tree in the twinkling of an eye and shouted down: 'Oh no! Anybody who wants supper with me must climb up and join me.'

So the poor old tortoise had to begin his long homeward journey with a very empty stomach, cursing his inability to climb trees. But, as he plodded along, he worked out a splendid plan for getting his own back on the devious baboon.

A few days later Baboon received an invitation to eat with Tortoise. Baboon was surprised. However, firm in his belief that Tortoise was slow-witted and good-natured, Baboon said to himself: 'Oh well! He evidently saw the humour in my joke and bears no ill feelings. I will go along and see what I can get out of him.'

At the appointed time, the baboon set out along the path that led to Tortoise's home. It happened to be the dry season, when there are many bush fires, which leave the ground scorched and blackened. Just beyond a stream the baboon found a wide stretch of burnt, black grassland. He bounded across it towards the tortoise, who stood waiting beside a big cooking pot from which drifted the most wonderful savoury aromas.

'Ah! It is my friend Baboon!' said Tortoise. 'I am very pleased to see you. But did your mother never teach you that you must wash your hands before each meal? Just look at them! They are as black as soot!'

The baboon looked down at his hands, and they were indeed very dirty from having crossed the burnt patch of ground.

'Now run back to the river and have a good wash,' said the tortoise, 'and when you are clean come back to join me for supper.'

The baboon eagerly scampered back to the stream, across the black earth, and washed himself thoroughly in the flowing water. But, when he got back to Tortoise, he found that, in crossing the burnt ground again, he had arrived as dirty as he was before.

'That will never do! I told you that you could only eat with me when you had cleaned yourself. Go back and wash again! And you had better be quick about it as I have already started my meal!' complained the tortoise with his mouth bulging. This wasn't very good manners, but it had the desired effect.

The poor baboon went back to the stream time and time again but, try as he might, he would get his hands and feet dirty again each time he returned across the burnt field, and Tortoise refused to give him any of the delicious food that was fast disappearing. At long last, as the final scrumptious morsel went into Tortoise's mouth, the baboon realized that he had been tricked. With a scream of rage, he ran across the burnt-out field for the last time, all the way back to his treetop home.

'That will teach you a lesson, my friend!' thought Tortoise, smiling to himself. And, well fed and contented, he withdrew into his shell for a long night's sleep.

Reptiles from ancient times

Leopard Tortoise
Geochelone pardalis

Tortoises, terrapins and turtles belong to a collection of reptiles known as the chelonians, a successful group that has remained almost unchanged since it began to evolve in the Triassic era – 210 million years ago! Its best-known feature is the shell: this strong armour is heavy, and so speed has had to be sacrificed – something that is reflected in nearly all folklore about the tortoise.

The Leopard Tortoise is the largest of the southern African chelonians, and specimens in South Africa's Eastern Cape Province may weigh over 50 kilograms, though it usually reaches only about 15 kilograms. These reptiles are found in a wide variety of habitats, except for dense woodlands and really dry desert areas.

The tortoise can live to 80 years. The female buries a clutch of 6 to 12 eggs in a hole in the ground and then leaves, taking no further care of them.

The young hatch during the next rainy season. Their sex depends on the average temperature at which they were incubated. Males develop at lower temperatures, females at higher temperatures – the exact opposite of crocodiles.

Though fossils of extinct chelonians have teeth, the tortoise has just a horny beak, somewhat like a parrot. As a result they have a diet restricted to vegetation such as flowers, leaves and succulents.

Our tortoise populations have been seriously depleted by 'pet trade' collectors, and many die in captivity in cold, wet climates.

The Shona

The forebears of the modern-day Shona were the Karanga people. They settled in what is now Zimbabwe and were large-scale cattle owners and skilled miners who worked the gold and iron deposits of the region. They were able to build sturdy stone dwellings (unusual in sunny Africa) and immense walled structures. The palace built for Mateya, wife of the great thirteenth-century Karangan king Chigwagu Rosvingo, for example, comprises nearly a million interlocking pieces of granite, each a perfect fit (mortar was unheard of at that time).

The stone houses were known as *dzimba dzimbabwe*, from which the modern country derives its name. The empire that developed was ruled by a paramount chief known as the *Madzimambo*, and it became a thriving centre of trade with (mainly) the coastal Arabs.

Its commercial connections actually extended further afield, even to central Asia, India and China. Later came the early Portuguese explorers, who arrived from the Mozambique seaboard in search of gold, ivory and slaves.

The Shona of today have inherited the values, traditions and many of the convictions of their forefathers. The extended family, and reverence for the ancestral spirits, remain central features of life, most notably in the rural areas. Contemporary Shona stone sculpture is world renowned.

Why Heron has a bent neck

A SHANGAAN TALE

One day Jackal went hunting and, as he was stalking through some outcrops, he spied a dove feeding its young in the rocks above him. Jackal knew he would be unable to reach the bird's ledge, which was high above his head, so he called out to the dove, 'I am hungry, little dove. Throw down one of your children for me!'

'I most certainly will not!' replied the dove.

'Then I shall fly up there and eat all of your children – and you too!' threatened the jackal. The bluff frightened the foolish dove, so she threw out one of her downy squabs. The jackal snatched up the youngster and ran off with it.

The next day the jackal returned to the dove and made the same threat. Again the foolish dove threw down another youngster. This one also disappeared down Jackal's throat as he trotted off, pleased with his deception.

The poor mother dove was distraught and her whole body heaved as she sobbed huge tears of sadness. As she was crying, a heron flew past, and then came down to her side and asked, 'Why do you weep so?'

'I shed tears for my poor babies,' sobbed the dove. 'If I do not give them to the jackal, he says he will fly up and eat me too!'

'You foolish bird!' scolded the heron. 'How can Jackal fly up here when he has no wings? You must not be deceived by such silly threats.'

So when the jackal visited the place again next morning, expecting an easy meal, the dove refused to part with her last baby. 'Heron told me that you cannot fly at all. You deceived me into sacrificing my precious babies!'

'That nosy heron!' the disappointed Jackal muttered to himself. 'I will pay him back for sticking his beak into other people's business, and for waggling his tongue too much!'

He trotted off and soon found Heron standing in the reeds at the edge of a pan, looking for frogs. Heron looked down his beak at Jackal as he approached, wondering what mischief he was up to today.

'What a wonderful long neck you have!' said the jackal in a most pleasant and complimentary way. 'But what happens when the wind blows? Does it not break in half?'

'No! I just lower it a little,' replied the bird, motioning what he did when the wind blew.

'But when the wind grows harder?' asked the jackal, feigning real concern.

'Then I lower it a little bit more,' responded the heron and showed Jackal how he could drop his head even further.

'And when it really blows a gale?' added the jackal.

'Then I lower it all the way to the ground,' said the heron, lowering his head and beak until they were level with the water's edge. Then the jackal sprang up with lightning speed and hit the heron's neck with all the strength that he could muster. There was a loud crack as the heron's neck broke in the middle.

Jackal ran off well pleased with the lesson he had taught the interfering heron. As for Heron, ever since that day he has always had a bend in his neck.

The lone grey fisherman

Grey Heron

Ardea cinerea

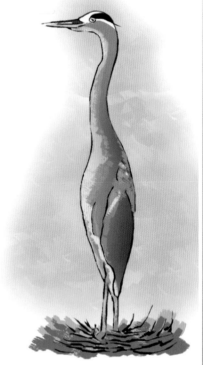

The Grey Heron occurs near fresh water throughout Europe and across Asia and Africa, nesting in large, noisy heronries and, in Africa, mixing with other water bird species. Males choose a nest site, usually picking the highest available spot. Females select a mate based on his choice of nest site. The successful male then collects nesting material and takes it back to the site, where the female builds the nest.

The heron is easy to identify in flight by the slow, deep wing-beats and the way it carries its neck curved in an 'S' shape, bent back against the chest.

Though it nests in colonies, the heron prefers to hunt alone. One of its nicknames is the 'lone grey fisherman' because of its solitary habits and its grey colouring. It is usually seen standing motionless in shallow water, or stalking around with stealthy, deliberate strides, clearly trying not to disturb its prey. It is an opportunistic feeder and, as a result, it enjoys a varied diet. Fish is the main menu item, but the bird will also take tadpoles, frogs, lizards, small snakes, invertebrates such as snails and water insects, small mammals, small birds (when they arrive to drink) and the young of other water birds.

A habit that annoys people with fish ponds is the heron's taste for expensive koi carp and goldfish, which are snatched from garden ponds and are obviously a delicacy on the heron's menu.

When Tortoise misled the Monkeys

A SOTHO TALE

One morning Tortoise was not very happy with himself. He felt the need to gorge on some wild bananas, but could not find any. Nearby, some hornbills were flapping around loudly, filling the air with their raucous alarm calls. They went: 'Tock, tock, tock, tocky, tocky, tock, tock!'

Tortoise really disliked these noisy birds with their ugly voices, so he decided to go down to the river and try to find some wild bananas in the cool, shady groves where he could relax and play his duiker-horn pipes. Maybe, too, he could have some fun at the expense of the crocodiles that usually sunned themselves along the water's edge. As he went, he played his pipes and, as the familiar tune of *Tswentswetle, tswentswetle* echoed over the hills, the grasshoppers and insect singers of the green grasses joined in the song.

An hour later the tortoise reached the crystal-clear waters of the stream and felt the cool, damp air in the shade of the acacia and fig trees. Tortoise decided he would rest up in a clump of reeds and just watch the comings and goings of all the animals and birds, for this was a popular watering place that all the creatures visited at some time or other.

Several huge crocodiles were basking on the sand banks and islands of the river. Little crocodile birds darted fearlessly in and out of the fearsome gaping jaws of these ancient creatures, acting as toothpicks to their seemingly ungrateful hosts. Tortoise relaxed in this idyllic spot and watched quietly.

A while later, one of the crocodiles waddled laboriously up the bank to the top of a mound and scraped away some of the sand to reveal a clutch of eggs buried in the nest. She left the nest open for a short while, covered it up again and then, hoping that she had not been observed, she slipped back into the pool of water.

Tortoise was delighted with what he had seen. Crocodile eggs! That was a valuable piece of information, one that he was sure he could exchange with his friend the vervet monkey in return for information on the whereabouts of some wild bananas, which he still hungered for. He knew that a troop could be found in a kloof nearby, so he crawled over to the kloof, which was not an easy task, for it was rocky and overgrown. As soon as he saw one of the monkey sentinels, posted to watch out for the safety of the troop, Tortoise started to play his famous tune:

Tswentswetle, tswentswetle,
Whose horns are these?
Tswentswetle, tswentswetle,
These horns are the bringers of good news!

Calling up to the monkey swaying in the lofty branches high above, Tortoise said, 'A good day and rewarding hunting to you, Kgabo. I bring good news to the leader of your troop. Would you be so kind as to convey to him that I desire to speak with him?'

The monkey climbed down and said to the tortoise, 'First tell me you are up to no trickery, Tortoise. Your cleverness and your deception go hand-in-hand! Any tomfoolery and you will suffer our wrath, and you will surely be torn limb from limb by our troop!'

Tortoise leaned forward and whispered in the sentinel's ear that he knew of a feast of crocodile eggs awaiting the monkeys' pleasure. But they must not delay for, even now, the eggs might be consumed by a huge python that the tortoise had seen coiled up in an ancient sausage tree close to where the eggs were buried.

With this inviting news, the monkey scampered off to fetch his troop leader, and when they returned the tortoise said, 'I know of your great weakness for eggs so I have stored a cache of them in the sand of the river bed so that they will remain fresh for you. In exchange for this information, I want to know where I might find wild banana plants, the food for which I have a particular weakness. I believe my request is a modest one!'

'We will give you bunches of wild bananas,' promised the leader of the monkey troop. 'That is, as long as you lead us to the place you stored the eggs, for speed is of the essence if we have to beat the python to the spoils! It is best that you ride upon my back!'

With that, the monkey scooped the tortoise up over his hairy shoulders and off they leapt through the tree canopy. This took Tortoise completely by surprise. He was most unaccustomed to being so high, and jostled and bumped around so much. He was soon feeling quite dizzy and ill. But it did not take long for the agile troop of monkeys to reach the river bank. The tortoise showed the monkey the site of the crocodile's nest, and the monkey gave Tortoise a huge bunch of wild bananas as his reward. The mischievous schemer slipped unnoticed into his hiding place in the reeds to watch events as they unfolded.

The monkeys raced up the river bank, chattering and pushing each other in their scrambling search for the crocodile's nest. One of them soon found the spot, and one by one the eggs were unearthed. The find prompted a noisy quarrel, and when one monkey threw sand into another's eyes a fight threatened to break out. There was great confusion.

To add to the chaos, the crocodile eggs began to hatch. Alarmed by the mayhem, the hatchlings nipped and snapped at the hairy fingers and toes that surrounded them. They also gave off their high-pitched alarm calls to attract the attention of their parents. And then there were howls and screams from the monkey sentinels to warn of the crocodiles' approach.

In a flash the parent crocodiles rushed out of the river, enraged to see the monkey troop tearing up their nesting site. With snapping jaws and slashing tails, they sent the swarming monkeys screaming and howling for the long grass and a nearby marula tree. The uproar was deafening. And for all the monkeys' frenzy they had not managed to escape with a single egg! The crocodiles were very relieved to find they still had their healthy babies, which the mother carefully scooped up into her mouth and carried down to the safety of the nursery area in a backwater of the river.

Meanwhile Tortoise, hiding in the reeds and munching on his favourite food, had thoroughly enjoyed the entertainment. He was very pleased with the outcome, and with his own clever deviousness. But he knew, only too well, that he would have to avoid that troop of monkeys for some time to come!

Living dangerously on the forest's edge

Vervet Monkey
Cercopithecus aethiops

This little monkey, with its distinctive black face and feet, grey fur and long, black-tipped tail, is found in a wide range of habitats along the edges of forests. This environment also attracts powerful predators, notably leopards, eagles and pythons. To counter these threats, the monkey has developed certain defences.

Their social system allows for more than one male in a group, which means more watchful eyes and a better defensive arrangement – but also greater competition and conflict. Evolution has therefore given the dominant, or alpha, male brightly coloured genitals – clear badges of rank, to which other males submit.

The vervet has evolved the beginnings of a language. A distinctive bark gives warning of an attack by, for instance, an eagle – what the threat is and from which direction – and they quickly take evasive action. Similarly a 'chutter' warns of a snake and will have all the adults standing on their back legs and surveying the ground. Young monkeys take about two years to learn the vocabulary, during which time they will often make mistakes.

The vervet has a very varied diet, which includes fruit, leaves, buds, seeds, insects and, occasionally, birds' eggs and fledglings.

The River of Tears

A SWAZI LEGEND

There is a legend among the Swazi about the creation of Popanyane, which means 'little river of the waterfall'. The legend is about a beautiful waterfall in a lovely valley – one that's treasured by the Swazi people. It is located near the Swaziland town of Pigg's Peak.

Long ago, a beautiful Swazi girl loved a handsome young warrior, who, in order to win her hand in marriage, was required to present her father with the skin of a leopard that he himself had killed. This leopard had to be killed on the slopes of the *Gobolondo*, 'the rugged mountain'. While he was undertaking this difficult task, the young suitor was captured by some witches who dwelt on this remote mountain. As he would not become their slave he was transformed into a white flower that grows amongst the grasses. Here he is doomed to live and grow and die each season with the grasses, as punishment for his trespass into the world of the witches.

Meanwhile, the beautiful young maiden waited in vain for her lover. When he failed to return, she despaired. She would sit on the banks of the Popanyane River and weep long and hard. So copious were her tears that eventually they formed a waterfall, which flows to this day, a living monument to her great loss.

The Swazi

The traditional Swazi are staunch believers in the ancestral spirits, or *Emadloti*, who are believed to appear as a small green snake that emerges from the base of the spine of a person shortly after death. These snakes bear tidings from the dead ancestors, messages that are translated by a *sangoma*, or healer. The ancestral spirits of the royal household look after the family as well as the entire nation.

The beadwork of the Swazi is world renowned. Originally the pattern of the beads served as a kind of love-letter from a girl to a favoured young man but, unlike a written letter, which is private, the beads declared her love to the whole world. The patterns varied from area to area, but the colour of a bead would be as specific as a letter in the alphabet.

Why we should listen to Squirrel

A VENDA TALE

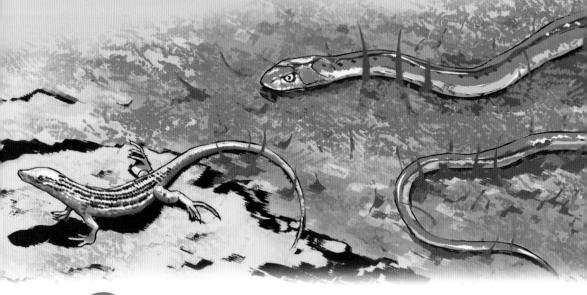

One day a small, green grass snake had caught a plump lizard and made a good meal of it. Then he looked around for a comfortable place to rest and found a nice, warm, sunny patch in some long grass, beneath a large tree. He was soon fast asleep in the warmth of this sheltered hideout.

Some time later, a tree squirrel was sauntering along the branches of the tree, when the sunlight that was sparkling on the scales of the little grass snake caught his attention. The squirrel began chattering and squeaking to himself as squirrels usually do when they see something bright or unusual. The longer it took him to work out what was making the sparkles, the louder his chattering became. It was not long before his chattering attracted the attention of a hunter who was walking along the track that passed the large tree.

'What can this be?' thought the hunter to himself. 'I wonder what has attracted the attention of my friend Squirrel today!'

Slowly the hunter walked to the foot of the tree, where he saw a little grass snake curled up sleeping in the sun with the light sparkling off his scales.

'So that is all that the noise is about!' exclaimed the hunter, rather disappointed that it was not something that he could take home for supper. 'A mere grass snake, which is neither harmful, nor good for the pot!' And the man crept away without waking the little snake.

But the squirrel carried on his incessant chattering and when another man came along the path he thought, 'I had better take a look and see what the squirrel is talking about!' He grasped his spear and stalked closer.

As soon as he spied the little grass snake he said in disgust, 'My wife would not thank me if I brought that home for supper. I had better not waste my energy on such a small one, especially as it is harmless!' He returned to the path and went on his way.

Now, while all this had been going on, a big spitting cobra had been hiding in the long grass nearby. He had not been having a good morning. In fact, he had been chased several times by some hunters, for not only was his venom deadly, but he also tasted good when boiled up in a cooking pot. He had managed to escape his pursuers for the time being, but he could never relax his vigilance, for someone was always ready to kill him.

When he saw the two hunters sneak up on the little grass snake and make no attempt to kill him, the spitting cobra decided that the patch of sunlight under the tree must be a magic place, a place where snakes would be left unmolested. So he uncurled himself and slithered over to the tree. As he approached, he raised his head and flared out his hood, spitting at the harmless little grass snake. The grass snake woke up from his peaceful sleep and, in terror, fled away into the bush.

'Psss!' said the spitting cobra to himself and he curled up on the exact same spot where the little grass snake had recently enjoyed his slumbers. 'Now I have the perfect place to sleep in peace!'

The squirrel had seen all that had happened, and had not ceased his constant chattering, but now it was louder than ever before. This did not bother the cobra, for he was used to the annoying jabber of the squirrel and his kind, who were forever dogging his movements.

Soon a third man came along the pathway. He was returning empty-handed from a disappointing hunt.

'What is this I hear?' he thought to himself. 'Squirrel does not make such a noise for nothing. He must have seen something interesting. If I follow his trail I may have something to take home after all!'

With silent footsteps, and with his stick raised, the man stealthily made his way to the foot of the tree. All the while the squirrel chattered noisily. Then the man saw the huge cobra fast asleep and defenceless, and he gasped in surprise. Swinging the club, he killed the serpent with one blow, picked it up and shoved it into his shoulder bag.

'Thank you, little squirrel!' the man called out as he departed. 'I should not have known that the snake was here had it not been for you.' He hurried home with supper for his wife and children.

But Squirrel, who had seen and heard everything, chattered and laughed even louder to himself.

'Now I see that what is safe for one creature is not for another. I must take heed of this lesson and never fall into that trap!' he said as he set off among the trees in search of his own supper.

Bright-eyed and bushy-tailed

Tree Squirrel
Paraxerus cepapi

This little animal is also known as the bush squirrel, yellow-footed squirrel and mopane squirrel, giving a good indication of its varied bushveld habitats. It is especially at home in savanna woodland and likes trees with holes in them, in which it makes its communal sleeping or breeding den. It also makes holes in the ground or in termite mounds. It feeds on the open ground, so it has to stay very alert.

Squirrels make an urgent 'chucking' call if they sense the approach of a snake or mongoose. When confronted, the squirrels will mob the predator. Rapid flicks of the long, bushy tail are also very clear visual signals employed when danger threatens.

Tree squirrels live in family groups. Territories are defended by the males, and are usually marked by scent. The animals also recognize each other by scent, sniffing nose to nose. The female has between one and three young after a gestation period of 56 days, which is exceptionally long for an animal so small.

The species feeds mainly on seeds, 'scatter-hoarding' what they do not immediately need beside grass clumps and around tree trunks, thus helping in the germination of tree seeds. They also eat insects, pollen, flowers and, on occasion, fledgling birds and eggs.

The tree squirrel varies in colour, tending to be grey in the dry western areas and becoming brown to reddish-brown the further east one goes, where tree cover increases. They love to huddle together in the warmth of the early morning sun, grooming each other before they start dispersing to find food for the day.

The magic horns

A XHOSA TALE

Once there lived a boy whose name was Magoda. He was an orphan, but the women of his village gave him food to keep him from starving, and in return for the food they expected him to run errands and to work for them morning, noon and night. The poor boy never had a moment to himself and, for all his labours, seldom did he get a decent meal. Life was an unending circle of collecting firewood, collecting goats and cattle for milking, and weeding gardens. Sometimes he was too tired even to sleep.

Eventually Magoda had had enough of this kind of life, and he made up his mind to end it by running away.

His only possession was an ox that his father had left to him before he died. The old man had told Magoda to take great care of the beast so one morning, before the sun rose, he crept to the cattle kraal. It was as if the ox understood the need for silence. Magoda jumped up on its back and the animal quietly walked away from the village, not stepping on sticks or the stones on the path or anything else that would make a noise.

And so Magoda escaped and took to the road, riding on the back of his ox.

On the way they travelled through villages with people going about their business. Nobody shouted at Magoda, or told him what to do, and he had a wonderful feeling of elation. On they went, but as the sun reached its zenith Magoda began to feel hungry and wondered where he would find food.

Suddenly a herd of cattle came into view and approached. In its midst was a fierce looking bull.

Magoda's ox spoke, saying, 'Get off my back. I will fight this bull and I will defeat it!'

So Magoda jumped off the ox's back, and it rushed towards the bull, driving it away from the cows. A furious fight developed, but this did not last very long, and soon the bull was dead.

'There now!' said the ox triumphantly. 'I have proved myself and my strength.'

So Magoda jumped back on the ox's back and they resumed their journey. But the boy was now very hungry and, as they passed another village, the smoke from the evening fires brought to their nostrils the smells of the evening meals. 'What would I not give for a good meal?' he said with longing.

To emphasize these words, he smacked the right horn of the ox and, to his amazement, food began to pour from the horn. Beans, pumpkin, mielie meal and meat, all cooked to perfection, flowed forth, and he grasped the gifts with both hands and pushed them into his mouth. The food came out so quickly and in such abundance that much of it fell to the ground.

'This is wonderful!' exclaimed Magoda, and smacked the left horn with

his hand. The right horn stopped yielding food, and that which he had not consumed disappeared back into the left horn.

'So that is how it is!' laughed the boy. 'Thank you, good ox! My father truly did look after me that fortunate day he gave you to me. By striking your right horn I need never go hungry!'

They continued along their way, but as the sun set they came upon another herd of cattle. This time the ox gave a deep sigh and said to the boy, 'Here I must take leave of you! I have to fight this herd too, but they will kill me. When I am dead you must break off my horns and take them with you. They will provide for you at all times, whenever you speak to them, but they will never work for anyone else.'

'Please do not fight,' begged the boy. 'Do not leave me, for you are my only friend and companion.'

But the ox would not listen and made his way towards the herd. A fierce fight started and it looked as though the ox would win, but this time there were too many bulls for him to overcome and eventually he was killed, and the herd trampled over his body. Sadly, Magoda took off the horns, hid them under his threadbare cloak and went on his way.

It was not long before he came to another village, and the people there were singing a sad song of hunger. Drought had left them with little food and starvation stalked the land. Magoda believed that his horns could help bring some laughter back to this cheerless place – that is, if they were still fruitful now that they were no longer attached to an animal.

'Greetings!' he said as he strode into the village.

'Greetings,' some of the people replied. 'If it is food and lodgings that you want, young man, then there is nothing in this place of hunger.'

But one of the villagers kindly invited Magoda to his home to shelter for the night. Later, he took out his horns and hit one, saying, 'Give me food!'

Just as before, the bounty gushed forth from the horn. The people of the house were amazed and began to eat their fill at once. When they saw that the supply seemed to be endless, they invited their friends and neighbours into their home, and all had a fine meal. Never had so much splendid food been seen, and nobody went to bed that night with an empty stomach. When they were done, Magoda struck the other horn and the food that was left disappeared.

The boy had had an exhausting day and was soon fast asleep, but his host had seen him strike the horns and command the food to appear, so he knew they possessed great magic. The man kept watch over Magoda and, when he knew the boy was fast asleep, he crept out of the hut to the rubbish pile and rummaged around until he found a pair of ox horns. He then returned to the hut and silently stole the magic horns from Magoda's side, replacing them with the worthless ones. Magoda woke up none the wiser.

In the morning, Magoda bade farewell to the people of the village and set off on his travels again. He wanted to get as far away as possible from the kraal he had grown up in, from the people who had been so unkind to him. By midday he was hungry again so he struck a horn and said, 'Give me food.' But nothing happened!

'I must have struck the left horn instead of the right one,' he said to himself, and struck the other horn. Again nothing happened. So he studied the horns, and on closer inspection he saw that they were smaller than the horns from his father's ox. He knew he would have to go back to the village where he had spent the night and seek out the thief.

He waited outside the village until dusk drew in, and then he quietly made his way to the hut where he had slept. As he crept up he almost laughed aloud, for he could hear the impatient householder shouting over and over again, 'Give me food! Give me food I say! Do you hear me? Give me food!'

Magoda remembered what the ox had told him when they parted (that the horns would work for no one else). So he waited, and it was not long before he could hear the sound of the horns being thrown against the inside wall of the hut. Then the man stamped out, and Magoda slipped quietly in and found the magic horns, replacing them with the useless ones. He ran away swiftly, determined that he would now guard the horns with more care.

That night Magoda had another fine feast and slept in the branches of a tree so as to be safe from the wild beasts that prowled the darkness. In the morning he was again on his way, and at the first village he came to walked boldly in and asked the headman, an ugly person, if he could shelter there for the night.

'Go away! We do not take in beggars here! It is difficult to feed our own mouths without providing for worthless ones such as you!' the headman shouted.

Magoda agreed that he did indeed look unkempt in his threadbare and ragged clothes and cloak, so he left the village and went to a nearby river. He wondered if the horns would provide him with gifts other than food, so he struck one horn with the other.

'Give me rich clothes, oh Horn!'

To his great surprise, he saw finely woven cloth and ornaments appear from the horns. He put on these fine garments, and, when he had done so, he looked like a wealthy young man. He decided to return to the village.

This time, he received a welcome reception. Children stopped and stared. Young men went out of their way to ask what they could do for him. Maidens working at their homes smiled as he walked past. One young girl was exceptionally beautiful, so Magoda sought out her parents and they gladly offered him room in their home.

Time went past and Magoda produced food and wealth for all in the village. He was greatly respected by the people, and, when he asked the father of the household, the man readily agreed to Magoda's marriage to his beautiful daughter. The young couple were able to provide themselves with all the things they needed for a joyful home. Oxen filled the kraal, servants worked the fields, and children blessed the house.

And so Magoda found true happiness, and he and his wife lived a long and contented life to a ripe old age – thanks to the magic horns of the ox his father had given him.

The tokoloshe

The *tokoloshe* is a mythical creature who features in the beliefs of many of southern Africa's traditional cultures. He is generally described as small, ranging from knee to waist high, of squat, stocky build, with flat hairy ears, small black eyes, small hands and feet, and a covering of fine ochre-coloured body hair. He lives in the wild, usually in rocky areas and by river banks, and is able to make himself invisible to adults but not, apparently, to children.

The *tokoloshe* are not inherently evil, but if sorcerers capture them – and this is usually accomplished by taking advantage of their greatest weakness: their love for milk – then they will use the *tokoloshe* to carry out their evil purpose. In this even the *tokoloshe*, under cover of darkness, will sneak into huts and leave evil charms in the thatch or sprinkle poison on the victim's food. It may even deposit vile concoctions in the local stream, just above where the victim will usually draw his or her drinking water.

But left to his own devices, the *tokoloshe* would be just a mischievous prankster, actively seeking the company of children in order to play and generally have fun. No doubt many naughty childhood pranks are blamed on the presence of a *tokoloshe*.

The power of Tawana, the lion cub

A TSWANA TALE

The lion cub, Tawana, is the totem (a mystical symbol) of the BaTawana clan of the BaTswana, and this tale shows how powerful the totem is and how dire the consequences can be for those who break its laws.

Long ago there were a BaTawana man and his wife who longed for the blessing of children. However, the happy sounds of a growing family never broke the silence and solitude of their hut. After many sad years, the woman went to her husband and told him that at last their wish would be fulfilled.

'Through all these long years as man and wife, I have loved you,' her husband told her in response. 'But from this time onwards our love will be doubled. And on the day that you put a child in my arms, I will grant your greatest wish, no matter what it may be.'

The months passed, and the woman duly presented her husband with a fine, healthy baby boy. Now their happiness was complete. But a shadow of doubt crept into the mind of the woman: she decided she would have to test the love of her husband.

'Husband!' she declared, 'I have given you the man-child that you so desired. Now I remind you of the promise you made to me. My wish is that you bring me the liver of a lion so that I may eat it!'

'But where would I find this thing?' asked the man, somewhat afraid at the thought of having to kill a sacred lion.

'Then your promise means nothing!' exclaimed the woman, looking sullen. 'You do not love me at all!'

The man was deeply hurt by his wife's cruel words, and determined to grant her wish no matter what the cost might be. For days he pondered on how he could undertake such a dangerous quest. Finally, he decided that guile was the only way to overcome the power of the lion.

Then he saw the old lion skin that lay in the rafters of his hut. 'I will use that skin,' he thought, 'to disguise myself. I cannot hope to match myself against a full-grown beast so I must try to take a cub. My wife did not mention how big the liver should be!'

The next day he took the lion skin and some *ditloo* nuts to eat on the trek, then he set out for the nearby forest, where he knew that a pride of lions lived. It was a long search but eventually he found the pride fast asleep under the shade of a spreading fig tree. He threw a nut into their midst to test how deeply they slept, but none stirred. 'Good,' he thought to himself. 'I am fortunate, for they have eaten well, and they sleep deeply!'

So he covered himself with the lion skin, and, using some gut and a long thorn that he had brought with him, he sewed himself into the skin. When he had completed the task to his satisfaction he crept into the middle of the lion group and lay down among them, as if he, too, were asleep.

Later, when the lions awoke from their rest, they sprang up, instantly alert. They sensed the presence of a stranger in their midst. The man did his best to imitate their graceful, fluid movements, but his actions were clumsy.

One of the lions was suspicious, saying, 'This is no lion; it is a human!' The lion went closer and sniffed, but all he could smell was his own kind.

Another lion said, 'We can test him. It is well known that humans cannot eat stones as we can. If he is human we will soon know!'

But the man was quick-witted, and as soon as the lions began to crunch on stones he scattered the *ditloo* nuts on the ground and ate them as though they were stones. This satisfied the lions and they accepted him as one of their own. Time wore on, but the lions were still well satisfied from their recent feast so they continued to sleep through the afternoon and the night. The following morning they rose early and prepared for the hunt.

'I am sick,' said the man, 'I cannot hunt today as I would be of no assistance to you. I shall remain behind to look after the children.'

The suspicious lion once again grumbled, 'He is a human I tell you!' But the rest of the pride would not hear of it and he was left behind with the cubs. As soon as the pride was out of sight, he hastily killed one of the cubs and removed the liver. He left the rest untouched and quickly made his way home.

'See, my wife,' he proclaimed, 'I have granted you your greatest wish!' and he threw the liver to the ground at her feet. The woman was delighted with her husband's gift and promptly cooked and ate the liver. As soon as she had eaten the tasty treat, her throat became dry and parched, and then it burnt with such a fierceness that she thought she would die.

She called for water and her husband fearfully brought gourd after gourd to slake her thirst. But the more she drank, the thirstier she became. Eventually, in desperation, she went to see Phiri, the hyaena, who everyone knew was the greatest sorcerer in the area.

'You must find water from a deep, still pool,' said the hyaena. 'A pool that has never known Segogwane, the frog!' Then the hyaena laughed with his hideous call to the rising moon and was gone.

So agonizing was the woman's thirst that she could not wait for the morning and she hurried from stream to stream, but as she neared each one she heard the voices of many frogs, calling as if mocking her predicament. On and on she trudged through the night.

By morning, on the verge of collapse from thirst and fatigue, she came to a clear, still, silent pool. She sank to her knees and drank, and drank and drank. When she had finished, she was amazed to see that there was not a drop left in the pool; she had drunk it bone dry. In fact her stomach was so distended that she had to lean against a nearby tree, for she could not move for the weight of water.

Shortly before midday Mmutla, the hare, came for his usual drink, but seeing the pool was empty he asked, 'Where is our water?'

'My big stomach drank it!' replied the woman.

As nothing could be done about the matter, Mmutla thumped the ground loudly with his back feet and went off in search of water elsewhere, muttering his displeasure.

The next animal to appear was Tlou, the elephant. Fortunately for the woman he was not terribly thirsty, and when she explained why the pool was empty, he went on his way without much fuss.

Thakadu, the aardvark, arrived next. He badly needed a drink, as his meal of ants had been hot too, but there was nothing he could do, and he also went on his way, grumbling and not at all happy with the woman.

Khudu, the tortoise, was next. He had taken several days to walk to the water from the dry area where he lived, for his legs are very short and he walked slowly. Imagine his disappointment when he saw the pool bone dry, and he, too, with much complaining, turned away to find moisture elsewhere.

Kgabo, the monkey, came by, not so much because he was thirsty, but rather because he wanted to visit the other animals and listen to, and share, some gossip. He was followed by a whole procession of animals: Tshipo, the springhare; Phudu-hudu, the dainty little steenbok; Mosha, the ground squirrel. All the animals were most disgruntled to find that the woman had drunk their water. Tshipa, the civet, was probably most annoyed. Eventually, it seemed that no more animals were left to visit the pool, and as darkness drew in, the woman gave a sigh of relief, though she did not relish the hours of darkness ahead.

Her relief was short-lived. For out of the shadows strode Ntche, a big black and white ostrich. Amongst the BaTawana, many credit the ostrich with human-like powers. As the woman was about to hail the bird, to address him respectfully, he fixed her with a baleful stare and hissed menacingly, 'Where is our water?'

'My big stomach drank it,' whispered the woman in great fear, and she struggled to get to her feet.

'Well, I did not make your big fat stomach and I have come a long way to drink,' the ostrich said threateningly. 'And because I am thirsty I am not going away without it!' With that the huge bird lashed out with one of his big, strong legs and with a sharp toenail sliced open the woman's stomach. Out gushed all the water that she had gulped down so greedily, and flowed back into the pool, filling it once again.

Ntche took a long, deep drink, and, when he had finished, he went on his way, leaving behind the fallen woman. The ostrich was satisfied that he had given back to the animals what had been taken from them.

For many days the man waited for the return of his wife, but he waited in vain. He tended to the needs of his little son to the best of his abilities, but she never came back, for she had paid the price that one must if one ever transgresses the totem law. The hidden power of the totem had taken revenge for the lion cub, Tawana.

King of the wilderness

Lion
Panthera leo

Lions are the only truly sociable members of the cat family. They live in groups known as prides, consisting largely of females and their cubs, with a small group of males, usually close relatives. The young males are usually evicted from the pride when they are about two years old, and then wander the bush as nomads for several years until they are mature enough to fight for, and take over, an established pride from one or more other males.

At their nomadic stage juvenile lions usually form coalitions with other, often related, males of a similar age. The more they work together in a coalition, the better equipped they are to oust weaker males from a pride and, more importantly, hold onto their new position. These territorial battles are often vicious and sometimes deadly.

When new males take over a pride their first action is to kill the cubs. This will bring the females into season, and the new cubs will inherit the newcomers' genes – their way of ensuring that their genes, and not those of the evicted lions, will survive.

The females of the pride do most of the hunting, leaving the males to patrol and protect the pride's territory. When they are patrolling, the males cover great distances and roar continually to warn off nomadic youngsters or males from neighbouring territories.

The natural range of lions has been greatly reduced and today they are seldom found outside of conservation areas.

Tortoise and Lizard

A HERERO TALE

Tortoise had used up all of his salt and he found his meals tasteless and not to his liking. So he decided to call on his brother and ask if he had any to spare. Luckily his brother had plenty to spare.

'How will you take it back home?' he asked Tortoise.

'If you would be so kind as to wrap the salt in a piece of bark cloth, and then tie it up with some string, I could put the string over my shoulder and drag the bundle along the ground behind me,' said Tortoise.

'That is a splendid idea!' his brother exclaimed, and between them they made a neat package of salt. The tortoise set off on his long journey. The going was slow and the bundle went bump, bump, bump along the path behind him.

Suddenly, Tortoise was pulled up short, and, on turning around, he was surprised to find that a large lizard had jumped up on the parcel of salt and was just sitting there looking at him.

'Get off my salt!' shouted Tortoise. 'How dare you expect me to drag it home with you perched on top of it?'

'This is not your salt!' retorted Lizard. 'I was walking along this path when I found this bundle just lying there, so I claimed it and now it belongs to me!'

'What rubbish!' shouted Tortoise, 'You know very well that it is mine, for do I not hold the string that ties the parcel?'

But Lizard continued to insist that it was he who had found the parcel, and refused to get off the bundle – unless Tortoise would agree to go with him to see the elders, so that they could decide to whom the bundle belonged. No matter how hard Tortoise tried to argue his case, the lizard would not budge. So eventually Tortoise agreed, and together they went to the court of the elders.

Tortoise put his case first, explaining that, as his legs were too short, he always had to carry bundles by dragging them along behind him.

Lizard then dismissed the notion, saying that he had found the bundle lying in the road. 'Surely anything that is found lying in the road belongs to whoever finds it?' argued the lizard.

The elders discussed the matter at length, but many of them were related to the lizard and hoped that they might get a share of the salt. Eventually, they decreed that the salt bundle should be cut in two, and that each of the reptiles should get one half.

Naturally Tortoise was very disappointed, because he knew that the bundle was his. But he gave a resigned sigh, and the elders cut the bundle in half. The salt was divided between Lizard and Tortoise.

The lizard immediately seized the half given to him and took the largest

piece of cloth, leaving poor old Tortoise with a raggedy bundle. Most of his salt trickled out onto the ground. In vain were his attempts to gather the salt together with his stumpy little feet, and his piece of cloth was too small to hold it anyway. When he eventually got home he took with him just a fraction of his share, wrapped up in leaves and the scrap of cloth. Meanwhile the elders had gathered up the spilt salt, and, dusty though it was, they took it home to their wives.

Tortoise's wife was downcast when she saw how little salt her husband had returned with, and when he told her the story of how he had been dispossessed she was indignant at the way Tortoise had been treated. But it was done, and Tortoise was exhausted from his long journey. He needed several days of rest to recover. But this also gave him time to think and plan, for though Tortoise may be a slow mover, he has a cunning mind. Tortoise came up with a plan to get even.

Several days later, Tortoise said goodbye to his wife and plodded off down the path towards Lizard's home, with a gleam in his eye.

Some time later Tortoise saw the lizard, who was alone catching flying ants. When the lizard had had his fill of these delicious insects, he sprawled in the warm sand of the path and dozed. He did not hear the stealthy approach of Tortoise, who came upon him from behind, put his legs astride the lizard's prone body, and used the weight of his shell to pin the lizard to the ground.

'See what I have found!' Tortoise called out loudly.

'What on earth are you doing?' queried the perplexed reptile, awoken so rudely from his sleep.

'Well, I was just walking along the path when I found this "thing" just lying in the way!' explained Tortoise. 'So I picked it up and now it belongs to me, just as you picked up my salt the other day!'

The lizard wriggled and demanded that Tortoise set him free, but his captor insisted that they go to the court and let the elders judge. This they did.

Again the elders listened to both sides of the argument, and then one of the white-heads said, 'If we are to be fair, we must give the same judgement that we gave concerning the salt!'

'Yes,' agreed all the other old ones, 'and we had the bag of salt cut in two. Therefore, we should cut the lizard in two and Tortoise can have half!'

'That sounds fair,' said the tortoise, taking a knife from one of the elders. But the petrified lizard was too swift for the lumbering tortoise: the flashing knife severed just his tail, and he made his escape.

Lizard was never seen in the area again, fearful that Tortoise would want the rest of the half that was adjudged to be his. And Tortoise never got his full half, but this did not concern him greatly, for he considered that he had had his revenge on the greedy lizard.

To this day Lizard can still lose his tail in moments of great danger, feeling that a small sacrifice is better than paying the greatest one! But, luckily for the lizard, his tail can grow back, though it is never as fine as his original tail.

The lizard with the decoy tail

Western Striped Sandveld Lizard
Nucras tessellata tessellata

This species is one of five in the sandveld lizard family that have adapted to the arid savannas of southern Africa. Their rounded snouts, tubular bodies, and very long, colourful tails easily identify them.

They spend long periods underground, mainly to avoid the heat of the day. Surprisingly for such a small reptile, they specialize in hunting scorpions, actively searching for the burrows and then digging out their highly poisonous prey.

As they hunt on the surface of the soil, where they are vulnerable to attack from birds and mongooses, it may seem surprising that they aren't camouflaged. But there is method in the colour scheme – the bright red tail is a highly visible decoy, which predators usually attack. The lizard then simply sheds its tail, which writhes around independently. The head and body remain unharmed and the lizard can escape to fight another day. The tail will then grow back.

Most hunting and foraging is done in the early morning and evening, often around termite mounds after rain when the alates, or 'flying ants', emerge, and the lizards gorge on the sudden bonanza.

The Herero

The Herero are thought to have originated in North Africa, but migrated southwards where they would have intermingled with the Bantu-speaking peoples who were also shifting southwards. They spent some time living around the Great Lakes region of East Africa, and their folklore hints at a vague recollection of this period. Later still, they drifted even further south and into modern-day Angola and then westwards to the Atlantic coast. This westerly movement was probably dictated by the need to secure good grazing for their cattle, which represented the wealth of both tribe and individual.

The Herero are strong believers in the power of the ancestral spirits and their role as influential guides and guardians of living people's welfare. The head of each family is also a kind of priest, and something of a historian too: he can name all the family ancestors dating back ten generations. He can also ward off evil spirits by communing with the ancestors. The observance of the taboos, or *zeri*, is of vital importance to the wellbeing of the family and the clan.

The 'traditional' costume of Herero women is a long, colourful dress and a wide hat, a style that was actually borrowed from the wives of the early white missionaries.

Most of the Herero live in Namibia, but a small group did migrate to the east and settled in the region of Lake Ngami in neighbouring Botswana. This exodus occurred in the early 1900s, and followed brutal repression by the German colonists after a Herero rebellion. About three-quarters of the Herero nation lost their lives in this terrible period.

Singisi and the Mamba

A NDEBELE TALE

ong, long ago, according to the elders, the snakes had no master. Snakes ruled over all the other creatures of the bush, and all lived in fear of their dreadful venom and their wickedness. None dared stand up against the snakes.

Of all the early creatures, those who suffered the most at the hands of the snakes were the bird people. There was great slaughter among the birds of the bush, and their numbers began to decline. Not only did they suffer from snakes' fondness for their eggs and fledglings, but also their power to hold victims transfixed by their gaze, leaving them helpless against their wickedness.

The birds banded together and held an *indaba*, or meeting, of the greatest urgency. The feathered ones discussed what they could do to save themselves from the evil power of the snakes and, after much argument, they agreed that they must make war on the snake people, or 'belly crawlers' as they called them. Banding together in bravery could be their only hope of survival.

As you may guess, the legless ones had a great advantage over the bird people in battle, for despite their speed and agility in flight and their ability to drop swiftly from great heights, the birds were still not able to match the powerful venom of the snake. Through many contests, the snakes had won, time and again.

A day came when it seemed the snakes would win a final victory over the birds, when, unexpectedly, there came a battle cry from over a nearby hill.

'OOOP-OOOP-OOOP!' boomed the deep, resonating call, and out strode Singisi, the ground hornbill, together with three of his kin.

The snake people cowered, for the fearsome reputation of Singisi preceded him. All knew of the speed and strength of his sharp beak.

First to one side and then to the other, the beaks of Singisi and his kin flashed and darted in and out. The bodies of the snake people were tossed this way and that, with their necks neatly severed. The tide had turned in favour of the feathered ones and a great hiss of fear came from the snake camp.

And as if in answer to their hissing call, skimming over the top of the long grass as if he had wings, slithered the most deadly of them all: the dreaded Black Mamba, king of the snakes. He had come to lead his people in the final battle.

With two strikes, as swift as lightning, the Black Mamba sank his fangs into Singisi's brothers, killing them instantly. He then slowly approached Singisi and his wife, with a wicked gleam in his eye. Why should he hurry when he had the big birds at his mercy? Why should he move quickly, when he could bide his time and kill them at his leisure?

'*Now* who is lord of all things?' hissed the serpent menacingly. 'Now I will take revenge for those of my kind that you have slaughtered.'

The bird that sounds like a lion

Ground Hornbill

Bucorvus leadbeaterii

The Ground Hornbill is the largest member of the hornbill family, of which there are many species in both Africa and Asia. They are the only hornbills where a female will have more than one male partner; two or three partners, even four, will accompany the female, although she mates with only one.

Unusually for the hornbill family, this incubating mother does not seal herself in a hole in a tree trunk for protection against predators. All the males bring her food and share in the incubation and feeding of the offspring. The female lays two eggs, of which only one fledgling usually survives. The chick develops slowly – it remains in the nest for nearly three months – and even when it joins the older foraging birds, they carry on feeding it until it is nearly a year old. This is the longest known fledging period for any of the world's birds.

Ground Hornbills spend most of their time on the ground, and roost in trees at night. They are usually seen strutting around looking for food, which can include insects, beetles, lizards and rodents, birds' eggs, young birds, and even large, poisonous snakes.

They have most unbird-like calls, one of which is a deep, low-pitched 'ooop-ooop-ooop' that greets each new day. Sometimes the whole group takes up the call and, though not especially loud, it carries a long distance. Some say it sounds more like a lion than a bird.

Another unique feature in the Ground Hornbill's life is that it deliberately sets aside 'play periods' – the only bird known to do so. A youngster may pick up an object, signalling a play session that can last an hour or more, and which may involve the entire family group.

But Singisi's courage did not falter that easily and, with snapping beak and blazing eyes, he turned on the great mamba and called out loudly so that all who survived could hear: 'Why should the feathered ones be beaten by you? You are no better than a worm – you have no wings or legs and can only crawl on the earth!'

But, still, the odds were very much against Singisi. With only two of his family left alive – he and his wife – who would be left to carry on the fight?

Singisi lifted his great bill to the sky, to his ancestors, and sounded his resonating boom, 'OOOP-OOOP-OOOP!' which was followed by the smaller voice of his wife.

As the last sound left his beak, there came a deafening whirring of wings, and from high in the great blue dome swooped a pure white hornbill of great and dazzling beauty. Straight at the mamba the Ancestor of Singisi flew and his sharp beak sliced the snake into small pieces and he scattered them far and wide across the battlefield. As soon as his task was completed he rose back into the heavens and disappeared as suddenly as he had come, never to be seen again.

Ever since then, not even the deadly Black Mamba has dared to face Singisi, King of the Birds. Even today you will see Singisi striding through the bush, seeking here and seeking there, always searching for the snake people, never forgetting the day the mamba killed his brothers and always seeking to avenge them.

The Ndebele

The Ndebele originated as a clan of Nguni people who live in South Africa's present-day KwaZulu-Natal. The Ndebele were led by Mzilikazi, who had been one of Shaka's best young lieutenants. After leading a war party on a successful raid, he kept the captured cattle instead of sending the booty back to Shaka. This was tantamount to treason, and an *impi* was sent to find and kill the traitors. Learning of Shaka's wrath, the entire clan fled into the interior. In their quest for land, they finally trekked across the Limpopo River into what is now Zimbabwe, where for a time they were known as the Matabele. Their capital, near the rugged Matobo Hills, was called guBulawayo.

A small section of the Ndebele remained behind in the region east of Pretoria, where they evolved a distinctive culture. Its most striking features are the colourful geometric murals that brighten homesteads, and the heavy metal necklaces, anklets and bracelets that the women wear.

When Hare tricked Serval

A HERERO TALE

ong, long ago the animals wanted to clear some of the bush away to prepare land to grow their crops. They had chosen a good site, one that had rich soil and was close to the river, which would be useful should they have a drought and need water to keep their crops alive. But the ground was covered with trees and shrubs, and rank with long grass. Before it could be hoed, the trees and larger bushes needed to be chopped down. But there were difficulties.

'Without an axe, we cannot chop the trees,' said Hare.

'And if we cannot clear the lands, then we cannot grow the crops,' said the warthog.

'And if we have no lands, we cannot grow the beans,' said the gemsbok.

'Nor the pumpkins,' said the ground squirrel.

'Nor the sweet potatoes,' added the yellow mongoose.

'We shall starve,' they all concluded.

'Where can we get an axe?' wondered the hare.

'Serval has an axe,' said the warthog, 'but I do not think he would lend it to us!'

'Not he!' sneered Hare in disdain. 'He is the meanest creature alive!'

'Maybe he would if we offered him some of the beans,' wondered the gemsbok.

Then everybody chimed in with an opinion as to what the serval might want in return, and an argument began. But to no avail, as they knew Serval would not eat any of the crops that they hoped to grow.

'I suppose we should simply ask Serval if he would be kind enough to lend us his axe!' said the tortoise. 'It could do no harm to ask.'

'It is the only thing we can do,' they all agreed.

After some more debate they decided to send the gemsbok, as he was the fastest. Gemsbok set off at a gallop, and the rest of the animals talked among themselves about the crops they were going to plant. It seemed as if hardly any time had passed before the gemsbok came racing back.

'He has agreed!' panted the excited gemsbok. 'Serval has agreed.'

'Has he?' The animals could hardly believe their good fortune. 'He is going to lend us his axe?'

'Yes! All we have to do is guess his secret name!' exclaimed gemsbok.

'O-o-oh!' The animals all gave a long, drawn-out groan at this announcement. For a long time they sat in a gloomy silence. Finally, the hare said: 'There is nothing for it! We will have to guess his secret name.'

'Yes, but how?' all the animals replied.

'Let me think,' said Hare and he put his head in his paws. 'Perhaps if we ... no, that will not work ... but maybe if we ...'

Hare muttered to himself for a while, and at last he looked up and said, 'Ah, ha! That may work! That's the idea! It could well work. I believe it is worth a try.'

'You have a plan?' asked all the animals in unison. They could tell from the look on his face that Hare was hatching a scheme.

'I do not know. It may work, but it certainly is worth trying,' the hare said again. He spoke slowly and deliberately. 'What we must do is go out into the bush and find one of Serval's bird traps, and if we find a bird we must take it out. Then we must go to the river and find one of his fish traps with a fish in it. We take out the fish and place the bird in it and then take the fish and place it in the bird trap. Then we shall hide and wait till Serval comes to check his traps this evening.'

'I do not see what good this can do,' said the ground squirrel, voicing the opinion of many of the assembled animals.

But the hare simply grinned and said, 'Wait and see!'

So the animals went off down the track that led to the river. On the way they came across a dense patch of scrub beneath a large and spreading marula tree. This was where Serval had made a cunning trap of twigs and twine. Caught in the trap, with one of its red legs held fast, was a foolish young francolin.

Francolin was fluttering around in a most agitated manner. 'Set me free,' he cried as soon as he saw the animals approach. 'Please set me free and I will do anything you want!'

'You could be a great help to us,' said the hare, and he told the francolin of the garden they hoped to prepare and that they needed the help of Serval, but that Serval had set a condition for the loan of his axe. 'I want you to come with us and let me put you in a fish trap!'

'Oh my!' exclaimed the francolin in great alarm. 'If I do that, I will be killed!'

'No,' reassured Hare, 'my friends and I will see that no harm comes to you.'

'Well if you are quite certain ...' The francolin sounded less than sure, but it would certainly help him out of his present dilemma.

Hare nodded, set the francolin free, and together they all walked on down the path to the river. It did not take them long to find the fish trap and there, inside it, lay a large, shiny tilapia (which is a bream). The hare took it out carefully and then put the francolin in the trap so that only his red legs were in the water. Then hare told the tortoise, warthog and ground squirrel to hide in the reeds and watch to see what would happen.

'And make sure that no harm comes to our friend the francolin!' he shouted as he wrapped the fish in some wet grass and hurried off with the gemsbok to the snare in the bush. When they got there, they set the shining silver fish in the noose, then hid themselves in the long grass and waited.

Some time later they heard voices approaching and they froze in readiness, just as Serval's two sons strolled into view, their long, sinuous bodies gleaming like burnished copper in the dappled sunlight beneath the marula tree.

'Beneath the marula tree,' one was saying to the other. 'Father said it would be under the marula tree. Yes, there it is! There's something inside!'

'Look! Look! A fish!' the other young serval squealed in amazement. ' By the secret name of *Njusi*, our father, how can such a thing be?'

Hare and gemsbok could hardly breathe for excitement.

'A fish in a bird trap! It is not possible! This must be sorcery!'

'Do not touch it!' The serval's sons were very afraid. It showed in their fierce eyes and in the way their whiskers twitched in agitation. 'Let us get away from here!' With a final anxious glance at the innocent silver fish, the young servals ran off down towards the river.

Hare and Gemsbok were jumping with glee at the thought that they had found out Serval's secret name. 'Did you hear that?' they giggled. '*Njusi* must be his secret name. Now he will have to lend us his axe!'

The warthog, ground squirrel and tortoise were feeling bored and uncomfortable sitting in the prickly reed bed when suddenly they heard the serval brothers come racing down the path towards the river bank.

'Look!' cried one of the young servals as they skidded to a halt in front of the fish trap. 'Look! A francolin in the fish trap!'

'By the secret name of our father, *Njusi*, how can such a thing be?' the young servals exclaimed with horror. 'Our traps are bewitched! Aiyee! Aiyee! What shall we do?'

'Let us get away from here before any worse things befall us. Let us go home and tell our father of these signs!' And the servals ran away in terror. Tortoise, the warthog and the ground squirrel were also frightened, but only that they would split their sides with laughter! Then they jumped up and down with joy as they went to the fish trap and released the francolin.

The next day, the animals gathered at the ground they hoped to clear for their crops. At the agreed-upon time, Serval arrived, with his sons behind him, carrying the axe. The serval brothers were clearly unnerved by the events of the previous day but they did not dream that Hare would be able to guess their father's secret name. They walked into the crowd and all gathered around as Hare and Serval stood face to face.

'Oh, Serval,' Hare said in his loudest and most ceremonial voice, 'you have promised that you will lend us your axe if we can guess your secret name.'

'That is so,' replied Serval, 'and I shall keep my word!'

'Is it perhaps *Shitonga*?' (which means 'Cheetah')

'No!'

'Is it perhaps *Ngwi*?' (which means 'Leopard')

'No!' smiled the now confident serval.

'Is it perhaps *Njusi*?'

Now Serval was speechless and could just stare at Hare. The serval's sons now gave out a huge groan. 'Hare knows our father's secret name! Our traps are bewitched! Our powers are gone! What will become of us? Aiyee! Aiyee!'

'When you give us the axe, the spell on your traps will be broken. I, Hare, who knows your secret name, have said so!' Hare spoke with so much authority that he even impressed himself.

At length Serval said, 'It shall be as you say – the axe is yours.' The young serval handed the axe to Hare and the cats left in a daze, wondering if the curse had indeed been lifted from them as Hare said it would. But, from then on, their bird trap only ever caught birds and the fish trap only ever caught fish, which goes to show that Hare's magic must be powerful indeed! At least that is what the servals thought!

After the cats had left, the other animals cheered Hare and praised his cleverness. Then Hare took the axe, tested its sharpness and, after a sideways wink at his accomplices, the tortoise, gemsbok, warthog and ground squirrel, he began to fell the first tree in their new lands.

This is how Hare tricked the serval, and how the animals got their new lands.

The cat that catches birds in flight

Serval
Felis serval

The serval is a solitary member of the cat family. It prefers open, well-watered grasslands and mountain pastures, and is, therefore, a threatened species, for these are the very areas that are settled and planted by humans. It is quite happy to live on cultivated land and adapts well if the crops grown encourage rodents, which are its favourite food. This, of course, can be a help to farmers. But it raids chicken coops, too, and is persecuted as a result. It also suffers from the trade in pelts, which are still sought after for ceremonial attire.

This slenderly built spotted cat has a short tail and large ears. It locates its prey with its acute hearing. It is famous for the agile way it hunts – it pounces in most spectacular fashion and the swat of its paw is lightning fast. Amazingly, it can swat birds out of the sky by leaping several metres into the air.

The serval has a fairly large territory and its boundaries are likely to overlap those of several other cats. Males use their droppings (or scats) and their urine to scent-mark their home ground and thus avoid unwanted contact with others. The female will bring up her litter of one to three kittens on her own and stay with them till they are about a year old, at which time they move off to live a nomadic existence, before establishing their own territories.

The Bride of the Rainbow

A SHONA TALE

 nce, in an old place in an old time, it fell to the honour of Chibuta and her family that she sacrifice herself as a bride to the mighty, rainbow-cloaked Rain Lord, Lesa.

Chibuta was not the first such bride, for every year one of the prettiest of the maidens of the BaSango clan would leave the village at dawn and prepare herself during the day for her bittersweet sacrifice. Each evening there would be the sign of thunder and lightning coming from the Lord Lesa's abode high in the heavens. This was the harbinger of the rains, the sign that the Rain Lord was satisfied with the previous season's sacrifice.

The bride-to-be would cast herself into the mighty *Mosi-oa-Tunya* waterfall on the Zambezi River, which was sacred to Lord Lesa. The following morning, after Lord Lesa had devoured his bride in a single love-embrace, the Rainbow

Children would fill the sky around the great waterfall and they would hear the last moans of the bride through the surging storm winds that filled the turbulent chasm.

On the day of the ceremony, Chibuta put rattles on her ankles and adorned herself with beads and ornaments so that she could perform the ritual dances and songs. But she cried, as did all the maidens called upon to sacrifice themselves to the Rain Lord, as she carried the pot of palm wine that was to be poured into the cauldron at the foot of the falls, before she, herself, followed.

As she made her way down the path to the drumming of the great *ngoma*, the ceremonial drums, and the chanting of the masked ngangas, she came upon an old woman who was trying to gather firewood.

'Would you help me collect firewood, my daughter?' the old woman asked. 'These old crippled limbs make the task difficult.'

'Certainly, mother,' replied Chibuta respectfully. She helped the old woman collect as much wood as she could carry. 'I would also help you carry this load home, mother,' she added, 'but I have a long journey to take this day.'

Chibuta had nearly forgotten her grief as she helped the old woman.

'Never mind, my daughter. Thank you,' the old woman cried as Chibuta lifted the heavy load onto her bent and weary back. 'For this, and for your other kindnesses, you will be handsomely rewarded.' Then the old woman disappeared as quickly as she had appeared.

Chibuta continued on her way, starting to sob once again, when she heard a bird in the branch just above her head.

'Nci-nci-nci!' went the bird, as it hopped among the lianas that festooned the trees in the rainforest. This was the most beautiful bird that Chibuta had ever seen. It was an astonishing scarlet colour and had long, shiny tail feathers.

'Why do you weep, Chibuta?' asked the little bird.

'Why shouldn't I weep, little bird? I am doomed to die so young – am I not allowed some tears of grief?' And she told the bird her sad tale.

'Dry your tears, little one!' said the bird. 'No harm will come to you. The

Rainbow Lord is not the evil being that you think he is. Our Lord Lesa loves his brides and he decrees that, in order to live in the sacred palace in the heavens, they must give up the evil ways of the world. Only good laws exist up in the heavens. But none have so far obeyed the laws of the heavens and he has had to devour them. Had he not done so, no rain would have fallen on the earth and the Rainbow Children would be no more!'

'But how can I know the laws of heaven when I am only mortal?' asked the girl.

'You already know them, little sister, for you have been kind to the mother of our Lord Lesa, the old lady you met on your path,' the bird replied. 'All the other girls scorned her, more concerned with their own problems and, like you, they did not recognize her. Now pluck one of my tail feathers and it will guide you through your perils.'

The little bird sat still as Chibuta plucked out one of the tail feathers and placed it in a band tied around her hair. She continued on her way, but the sky started to grow gloomy, as if a great storm approached. However, it was not a storm. A towering cliff loomed in her path and blotted out the sky.

'This is but a wall built by our Lord Lesa, to test you,' the little feather said in her ear. 'Tie me on your shoulder and I will help lift you over.'

This Chibuta did, and immediately she grew two powerful scarlet wings. Testing her new wings, she found she could fly with strong wing-beats – she soared high above the wall and alighted on the other side in a beautiful green valley.

'Pluck me from your shoulder now, little sister,' said the tail feather. Obediently, Chibuta placed the feather back in her headband and walked through the pleasant valley. Eventually she climbed a koppie and saw beyond it, to her horror, a field of serpents. The writhing bodies and flashing, forked tongues from the hideous heads made her shriek and recoil in fear.

But the feather said to her, 'Throw me among them!'

Chibuta did as she was told, but she was anxious. 'I am afraid to lose you. You may be devoured!'

'I shall fly back to you!' reassured the feather. The feather landed amongst the serpents and straightaway the field turned to a sea of scarlet and gold flame lilies. The little feather flew straight back to Chibuta and perched in her hair.

Eventually the girl and the feather reached the foot of Lord Lesa's abode. 'Here I must leave you, little sister,' he said. 'My Lord Lesa will take you by the hand now!'

'Farewell, friendly little feather. Pretty little feather, farewell!' she said as she made a circle of her arms and watched the scarlet feather float away as if it were a tiny red canoe on the vast blue ocean of the heavens. As she stood there with her arms in a circle, she was suffused by a radiant light, many coloured, as if by a Rainbow.

'Hail! Oh my Lord Lesa!' she cried as she fell forward respectfully on her face.

'My best-beloved, come with me,' said a soft, soothing voice, like the sound of the rain bird's wings and the patter of raindrops on the parched earth. A rainbow bore them up into the high heavens to their golden thrones in the home of the Creator, Mwari.

And there she sits to this day. The brave maiden who became the Lady of the Rainbow, Queen of Lesa, she who brings forth the *mwana wa murende*, the drops from the rainbow that give to Man the blessings of a fruitful earth.

The smoke that thunders

Victoria Falls

The Victoria Falls rank among the greatest of the earth's natural wonders. They form the world's largest curtain of water – 1 708 metres wide and 103 metres high. During the Zambezi River's peak flow (March–April) 545 million litres of water flow over the precipice each minute – four times Johannesburg's annual consumption.

The volume and power give rise to its Kololo name Mosi-oa-Tunya, which means 'the smoke that thunders'. To the Nambyan they are known as Chinotimba, which means 'the place that thunders', and the Zezuru call them Mapopoma, a word that imitates the sound of the cascades. Scottish explorer David Livingstone 'discovered' the Falls in 1855 and named them after Queen Victoria. 'Scenes so lovely,' he later wrote, 'must have been gazed upon by angels in their flight.'

On a clear day, the rising spray can be seen 80 kilometres away, and at night, when the moon is bright, an eerie lunar rainbow arcs across the gorge.

Glossary

ACACIA The family name for a common group of trees, widely distributed throughout the drier parts of Africa. The leaves and seed pods are nutritious food reserves for animals and humans.

BUSH A general term applied to areas of southern Africa that still resemble their original, uncultivated state.

CAMOUFLAGE The coloration or pattern of an animal that allows it to disguise itself against its background.

CARNIVORE An animal that lives by eating the flesh of other animals.

CARRION The rotting flesh of dead animals.

ENVIRONMENT The physical conditions and circumstances surrounding any living creature or plant that influence its existence and well-being.

GOURD The dried and hollowed-out shells of fruits related to the melon, widely used as water containers and drinking vessels.

HUNTER-GATHERER Nomadic tribes, such as the San, who live off the land, catching game and collecting wild berries, roots, grains and fruits.

KOPPIE An Afrikaans name used throughout southern Africa to describe a small hill.

KRAAL An area surrounded by a stockade or fence, for protecting either livestock or human dwellings.

MAMMALS A term for a group of animals that are warm-blooded, have milk-producing glands, are partly covered in hair and bear live young.

NGANGA A southern African term for a person who specializes in traditional tribal medicines and magic.

PREDATOR An animal that catches other animals for food.

PREY An animal hunted and killed for food by a predator.

REPTILE A cold-blooded, egg-laying animal with a scaly skin, including snakes, lizards, and tortoises.

SANGOMA A traditional healer who specializes in natural herbal remedies.

SAVANNA Extensive areas of natural grassland and only scattered tree growth.

SCAVENGER An animal that lives off the dead remains of other animals or plants.

SOLITARY An animal that lives alone most of the time.

SPECIES A group of animals or plants, with common characteristics, that are able to breed with each other.

TERRITORY An area used by an animal for feeding and/or breeding, often defended against others of its own kind and occasionally against other species too.

Bibliography

Arnot, K. 1962. *African myths & legends*. Oxford University Press, Oxford.

Bleek, WHI & Lloyd, LC. 1911. *Specimens of Bushman folklore*. George Allen & Co, London.

Branch, B. 1990. *Field guide to snakes and reptiles of southern Africa* (2nd ed). Struik, Cape Town.

Busomhill, G. 1960. *The sacred drum*. Howard Timmins, Cape Town.

Courlander, H. 1963. *The king's drum & other African stories*. Rupert Hart Davies, London.

Elliott, G. 1949. *Where the leopard passes*. Routledge & Keegan, London.

Hopza, AC. 1983. *Shona folktales*. Mambo Press, Gweru.

Illeron, WG, Quinn, PJ & Hilstein, PLS. 1990. *Complete book of southern Afican birds*. Struik Winchester, Cape Town.

Junod, H.P. 1938. *Bantu heritage*. Hortors Ltd, Johannesburg.

Kosova, M & Stanovsky, V. 1970. *African tales of magic & mystery*. Hamlyn Publishing Group, New York.

Lee, FH. 1931. *Folk tales from all nations*. George C. Harrap & Co Ltd, London.

Matthew, L & Hewatt, MDT. 1906. *Bantu folklore*. Maskew Miller, Cape Town.

Miller, P. 1979. *Myths & legends of southern Africa*. TV Bulpin, Cape Town.

Mills, G & Hes, L. 1997. *The complete book of southern African mammals*. Struik Winchester, Cape Town.

Parrinder, G. 1967. *African mythology*. Hamlyn Publishing Group, London.

Partridge, AC. 1973. *Folklore of southern Africa*. Purnell, Cape Town.

Phillips, M. 1961. *The bushman speaks*. Howard Timmins, Cape Town.

Rabin, P. 1953. *African folktales & sculpture*. Pantheon Books Inc, New York.

Savory, P. 1961. *Zulu fireside tales*. Howard Timmins, Cape Town.

Savory, P. 1962. *Matabele fireside tales*. Howard Timmins, Cape Town.

Savory, P. 1963. *Xhosa fireside tales*. Howard Timmins, Cape Town.

Savory, P. 1965. *Bechuanaland fireside tales*. Howard Timmins, Cape Town.

Savory, P. 1965. *Fireside tales of Hare and his friends*. Howard Timmins, Cape Town.

Savory, P. 1973. *Swazi fireside tales*. Howard Timmins, Cape Town.

Skaife, SH. 1976. *African insect life*. Struik Publishers, Cape Town.

Visser, J. 1979. *Common snakes of Africa*. Purnell & Sons, Johannesburg.

Copyright © in text, 2004: Nick Greaves
Copyright © in illustrations, 2004:
David du Plessis
Copyright © in published edition, 2004:
Penguin Random House (Pty) Ltd

Publishing manager: Pippa Parker
Managing editor: Helen de Villiers
Editors: Peter Joyce; Emily Bowles
Design concept: Janice Evans
Designer: Janice Evans
Cover design: David du Plessis
Illustrator: David du Plessis
Graphics: Jerry Tapsell
Proofreader: Thea Grobbelaar

Reproduction by Hirt and Carter
Cape (Pty) Ltd
Printed and bound in China by
Leo Paper Products Ltd.

Published by Struik Nature
(an imprint of Penguin Random House
(Pty) Ltd)
Reg. No. 1953/000441/07
The Estuaries, No 4, Oxbow Crescent,
Century Avenue, Century City, 7441
PO Box 1144, Cape Town, 8000,
South Africa

Visit us at
www.penguinrandomhouse.co.za
and join the Struik Nature Club
for updates, news, events
and special offers

First published in 2004

9 10 8

ISBN 978 1 86872 998 2
ePub 978 1 92057 268 6
ePDF 978 1 92057 269 3